Summer Love: Take Two

Summer Love: Take Two

A Paradise Key Romance

Shirley Jump

TULE
PUBLISHING

Chapter One

THE OCEAN WASHED in and out with the same *shush-shush* song that Lauren Webster remembered. Shells tumbled in the surf, dancing with the waves, pooling in the eddies. Seagulls circled the shore, waiting for a chance to nab a forgotten sandwich or an unsuspecting fish. Everything in Paradise Key was exactly the same as she remembered.

Except their group of five, once as inseparable and close as braided strands of hair, now broken and scattered. And down to four.

The shock and grief hit Lauren all over again like a sucker punch. She dropped to the sand and pulled her knees to her chest, holding tight until the pain in her lungs eased enough for her to breathe again. Lily—sweet, irrepressible, optimistic Lily—gone in an instant after some lawyer too busy texting missed a red light and slammed into her Prius.

This week, Lauren had gone to the funeral and said goodbye. Right now, none of it felt real, not being here, not hearing about Lily, none of it. If this was a job, Lauren would cover the whole thing with some kind of colorful ad campaign that made the entire awful event softer, easier to take, like a pretend Hollywood moment with a sunset and a few tears.

But it was real life. And real life sucked.

Lauren got to her feet, brushed the sand off her pants, then picked up her heels and made her way up the sandy path that led to the Paradise Key Resort. Loosely named, because the place had fallen apart in the years since her family used to vacation here. But still a prime destination along the Gulf of Mexico that just needed a little physical and marketing brush up to become something big.

And to become Lauren's saving grace with a job that was in an even more precarious position than the wind and storm-battered resort. On the plane ride here from New York, she'd had a thousand ideas for how to capitalize on Paradise Key's tourism, but now, being back here, smack dab in the center of her past, every one of those ideas had flitted away.

She needed to get a grip. Get back on track. Quit letting her empty life distract her. Once she had secured her position at work again, and proved to her father that she was committed to the company, it would all be fine. It had to be.

At the boardwalk, Lauren rinsed the sand off her feet, then slid on the black Louboutins. The navy Anne Klein suit fit a bit looser than it used to—stress made Lauren lose her appetite, not increase it—but wearing the one-button jacket and twill pants made her feel and look more powerful and commanding. A little self-marketing before her meeting with the tourism bureau in a few minutes.

In the car, Lauren touched up her eye makeup, checked her suit for sand one more time, then headed into downtown Paradise Key to a small office on the corner of 2nd Street, in the very back of the town hall. A sign outside the door in one-inch white plastic changeable letters said *Paradise Key Tourism Bureau*—or sort of said that, considering the sign was missing a D, E, and B.

This did not bode well.

Lauren pushed on the door, trying not to roll her eyes when the tiny silver bell above her head let out a happy tinkle. Inside the room, two green clunky metal desks leftover from the invention of the steam engine flanked either side of the wall. A faded "Come to Paradise Key" poster hung between them, the edges curling away from the pushpins holding it against the sheetrock. The dingy green tile flickered beneath sputtering fluorescent lights. The office to the far right read *Gary Higgins*, with a hand-lettered sign beneath that said *ON VACATION*.

A long, lean man had his feet propped on the desk on the right, the chair tipped back at a precarious angle. His beard fluttered with his rumbling snoring.

Lauren took a step toward the man, about to wake him, when a short heavyset woman with a pouf of carrot-orange hair came bustling out of the back room. The scent of cigarette smoke hung heavy around her, no doubt caused by the half-empty pack of Marlboros peeking from the pocket of her bright red floral dress.

"Well, what do you know. A visitor!" The woman put out a hand. "I'm Eloise Josephs, head of the tourism bureau and official greeter for the town of Paradise Key."

"Lauren Webster." She shook with the other woman, then nodded toward the twin desks. Rip Van Winkle had yet to stir. "Not too busy today?"

"We're never busy, but that's okay. I don't know what I'd do if it was busy. With Gary on vacation this week, it's just me and Merle here." She nodded toward the napping man. "And half the time, Merle is, well, Merle is…busy. He's on the town commission, too. Doesn't get much time to sleep, what with all he gives to the town of Paradise Key. I try to make him lunch every day. He hasn't been eating right since his wife died, don't you know, and we're a family here, that's what we always say, so I—"

"I work for a marketing firm in New York City," Lauren cut in before Eloise started the next half of her verbal saga. "And I wanted to talk to you and the town commissioners about a marketing campaign for Paradise Key. Help put this little town on the map."

"Well, honey, it *is* on the map. Right there." Eloise pointed at a map of Florida that hung above one of the desks. A bright yellow pushpin had been shoved in the general area of Paradise Key. "I don't know what some fancy New York firm could do for us that we haven't done for ourselves."

"Tourism dollars for Paradise Key are down thirty percent over the last ten years. That's a sizeable drop. By engaging in a marketing campaign—"

"Don't buy anything she's selling, Eloise. Lauren here can talk the pope into a bad decision faster than he can say *bless you.*"

Lauren stilled at the deep voice behind her. It couldn't be. Not after all these years. He'd said he was leaving town, off to become some hot-shot banker. Leaving town. Leaving her. Leaving them.

She did a slow pivot, and there he was. Carter Malone. Six feet of man and mistake. "Carter?"

"Hello, Lauren." He gave her the grin that had once melted her heart and made her believe in the impossible. "Small world to see you back here."

Holy hell, he looked good. He'd grown taller, broader and a lot more muscular. He had on faded jeans and a pale green button-down shirt open at the collar. His dark hair swooped across his brow, a little long and almost hiding his coffee-colored eyes. She swallowed back her surprise, and affected a nonchalant air. "I could say the same for you."

Eloise hurried into the space between them, like a mother hen separating her warring chicks. "Do you two kids want some snickerdoodles? I made them for Merle, but he said he can't eat too many. Gives him indigestion, poor thing. And he forgot his Tums again. I keep meaning to run down to the CVS and buy him—"

"No thank you."

"We'd love some," Carter said at the same time, overriding Lauren's words. "Two snickerdoodles and a cup of coffee between two old friends. We can sit down and catch up."

Eloise clapped her hands, and hurried off to the back room again. Merle kept right on snoring.

"Since when have we been friends, Carter?" Lauren said.

"Since we're eating Eloise's cookies." He leaned closer to Lauren and lowered his voice. "Eloise's cookies are world famous. She must really like you to offer you some. Oh, wait, no she doesn't, because she doesn't like strangers who come in and try to fancify our little town with swanky New York ad campaigns. So I think the cookies were actually meant for me. Me, she does like. Because I'm nice."

Lauren parked a fist on her hip. "For one, I'm not trying to fancify anything. I'm just here to help Paradise Key become all it can be."

He scoffed. "I know you, Lauren. Better than you think. So don't try to sell me like I'm some hapless teenage boy looking for the right cologne to make some girl in Algebra faint at my feet."

The mention of the ad campaign she'd directed two years ago took her by surprise. Was it just a coincidence, or had Carter followed her career? "How do you know about that?"

"It's on your LinkedIn profile."

"Have you been keeping tabs on me?"

"Nope. Just doing my due diligence. Whenever there's a shark rumored to be in the waters around here, I make sure to check it out."

Lauren bristled. She was far from a shark. She was here to help the town, not hurt it. And, well yes, help her career, too, but not for some money-hungry reason. For a second, she'd thought Carter still cared. She'd been wrong. Good thing, because she didn't care about him anymore. Not at all. "Since when are you the Paradise Key protector?"

"Since my father asked me to be."

A shadow crossed his face. Lauren opened her mouth to ask what he'd meant, when Eloise came hurrying back with her impeccable timing and a tin of cookies. "Here you go. You kids help yourselves to some coffee. There's a little sitting area out back that me and Merle set up for when things are slow. You're welcome to take a load off for a few minutes and just enjoy the sun." Eloise patted Carter's cheek. "I know you'll show this girl some Paradise Key hospitality. Carter here is my advisor. Sort of the Hand of the King, if you watch *Game of Thrones*. Do you? Merle and I love it, though we weren't too happy with what that terrible Cersei did last season."

As Eloise prattled on and on, comparing a town with a population of less than a thousand with fictional medieval kingdoms, Lauren debated staying put and trying to sway Eloise, but the older woman seemed blissfully unaware that Paradise Key had hit a tourism hiccup. Merle had yet to wake from his hibernation, which left—

Carter Malone.

CARTER SAT BACK in the Adirondack chair. He propped his feet on the wooden crate that served as an ottoman, in the "sitting area" that Eloise and Merle had carved out of the few feet between the back of the town hall and the dumpster. The tin of snickerdoodles sat on one arm of his chair, a Styrofoam cup of crappy coffee on the other.

And Lauren Webster standing eight feet away, pacing the small area like a panther waiting for a gazelle to come by. The Lauren he remembered had been lighthearted, fun, as ready to dash into the ocean as she was to kiss him under the boardwalk. This Lauren—this buttoned-up, stressed, clipped-tone woman—he didn't know. When Jenna mentioned the other day that Lauren was coming to town for the funeral, Carter had looked her up. Out of curiosity. Nothing more.

He'd expected Lauren would have settled down in some suburb with an accountant or something. She'd been so adamant about not wanting to work for her father when he knew her that it took Carter completely by surprise to see her listed as one of the "growing stars" at her father's marketing agency in New York.

The woman he had met years ago had been quiet and intelligent, but with a spirit that was straining against the structure of her life. When she'd shrugged off her father's rules for a few months that summer, she'd become someone he couldn't resist. Fun, bright, daring.

Then she'd gone to work with her father, and the career he saw had been successful—but built on bold marketing campaigns that took her clients from tiny to blockbuster. She was talented, that was for sure, but also known for creating out-of-the-box ideas that grabbed attention. He had no doubt that was the same kind of thing she planned for Paradise Key. She'd do some crazy off-the-wall advertising painting little Paradise Key as *the* spring break party destination—a technique he'd seen with the neighboring towns, and with the New England towns Lauren's firm had worked with over the years. Yes, the campaigns had brought in revenue, but also a higher crime rate that drove out the residents and left the town almost vacant in the off season.

That was the very thing he was helping the tourism board avoid. So that meant he didn't need to help her at all. He was just there for the cookies anyway.

"Are you in charge of the tourism bureau?" she asked.

"Nope." He pulled out the fattest, most cinnamony snickerdoodle in the bunch. Jackpot.

"A member of it?"

"Not officially." Eloise, however, trusted Carter's judgment, and often consulted with him. They'd started a charity project together a couple of years ago, and he'd been a de facto member of the tourism board ever since. Eloise had said more than once she liked that Carter's vision for Paradise Key matched her own.

Lauren paced some more, her brows knitted and her lips pursed. Tense Lauren needed the cookie sugar rush more than he did, but he wasn't inclined to share right now.

"Then why would I have to talk to you at all to get a marketing plan approved?"

He gave her a grin. "Because Eloise loves me. She and my father go way back, and she trusts my opinion when it comes to the town."

Lauren rolled her eyes. "That's not how a town is run. Or a tourism bureau."

"Maybe not." Carter took a bite of a snickerdoodle, then waved the cookie at Lauren. "You should have one of these. They're amazing."

"I'm not here for cookies, Carter. I'm here for business. This town needs to take advantage of the tourism dollars that flood Florida. The numbers are up three percent every year. In Broward County alone, tourists spent ten billion dollars. That's billion with a B. Paradise Key should take its part of that giant pie. Kickstart things around here."

"Why the hell would we want a kickstart?" Carter asked. "And why do you care what some teeny tiny town does for its marketing? Hell, you could walk into any restaurant in New York City and come out with a bigger advertising budget than we'd have in five years."

"True." She paused, clearly weighing her words before she spoke. "This would be a very small project, not exactly the kind McNally and Webster normally take on, but it's a start. An entry into the Florida market, which we have not worked with before."

Something didn't ring true with Lauren's answer, but Carter couldn't pinpoint it. Either way, he didn't want some big-city marketing agency putting their stamp on Paradise Key. "We're happy being a sleepy little town," he said. "One of those great unknowns."

"We? Since when are you part of the we? Last time I talked to you, all you wanted to do was get out of this town."

"I changed my mind." A hell of a lot more had kept him rooted to Paradise Key, but he didn't tell Lauren that. The days when she was his closest friend and the woman he loved had ended years ago. Albeit, at his choice. At the time, he'd thought he was doing the right thing for his life.

He glanced at Lauren's left hand. No ring adorned her finger. Not that Carter cared. Well, maybe he did. A little.

"Since when are you the career-driven girl?" he said. "Last I remember, you were going to drop out of school and live here."

"That was a foolish dream by a teenage girl who believed the lies her boyfriend told her." Lauren's face held less emotion than her words. "We all make promises we can't keep when we're young and stupid."

Touché. He couldn't blame her for the dig. After all, he had broken her heart. "I guess we've both changed since that summer."

"We've spent enough time out here," she said. "I'll go in,

tell Eloise I had a bunch of cookies, and then get her to sit down and talk about what my agency can do for the town. If it's at all possible, I'll get Merle Van Winkle there to come out of his coma and join in the conversation."

"You can't." He waved another cookie at her. "You haven't tried the cookies yet."

She rolled her eyes again. "I'm not eating the damned cookies."

"They're really good." He took a bite. Another. "Better than my mom's, and that's saying something. Remember her chocolate chip cookies?"

"Your mom made some incredible cookies." Lauren stopped pacing, and her gaze lit on him for a moment. "I remember that time she packed a picnic lunch for us. We took it down to the beach and—"

He knew why she'd ended the sentence. Because what came after that afternoon on the beach had changed everything between them. Carter and Lauren had gone from friends to lovers—not very good lovers, considering it had been the first time for them both—and their vacation romance suddenly got very, very real. And very, very serious. At least on Lauren's end. She'd begun to talk about leaving home and staying with him in Paradise Key. Ditching the college and the career and life her father had laid out for her practically since birth. Carter had been eighteen and scared as hell of any kind of binding tie. So he'd chosen what he thought would make him happy.

He'd been wrong.

For a while, Carter had everything he thought he wanted. A corner office and a promise of a promotion to CFO. A Mercedes. A penthouse apartment in Chicago. A fiancée who was as driven and serious about her career as he was. He was, as they put it, living the dream. Then he'd come home to Paradise Key to take care of his father. It'd made him realize his priorities had been backward for a long, long time.

The fiancée had stayed a week, then said she couldn't be with a man who thought like a small town. The job went to someone else who was willing to put in the hours and sacrifice the weekends. The apartment, furniture, and life ended up with the fiancée and her new husband. And Carter had stayed here, working in his father's store, settling into this town, and finally seeing what was most important.

It wasn't apartments or cars or titles. It was family and roots. The same things he had once run from, but now embraced with the maturity of someone who nearly lost it all. Seeing Lauren again made him think of that summer, of how she'd told him that she'd never felt at home until she'd come to Paradise Key. Was that woman still in there?

Carter pushed out of the chair and held the cookie up. She remained stony, still. "Take a bite, Lauren. Just one."

"I need to—"

He'd seen a flicker of the Lauren he remembered when she talked about the picnic. The Lauren he'd never forgotten. The Lauren he missed, more than he had realized until she popped back into his life. He searched her green eyes, waiting for the glint of a tease, the hint of desire. The playfulness that had kept him captivated that summer. Nothing. Just a cold flatness. "What happened to you?"

She blinked. "What do you mean, what happened to me? Nothing."

"You used to be fun. Spontaneous. Daring. Now you're all suited up and ready to go to war with a tourism bureau made up of a couple of retirees who spend their days knitting and napping."

"I'm doing my job, Carter."

"Killing two birds with one stone? Making the trip a tax write-off maybe?" What was in it for her? What could Paradise Key possibly have that Lauren wanted so badly?

"What do you care?"

"I care because one of your friends died, and you haven't once brought it up or wondered if I knew. You weren't the only one who was shocked at Lily's death, you know."

Tears welled in her eyes, and the icy cold dropped from her gaze. Damn. He'd gone too far. Pushed her too much. Taken his frustration and disappointment out on her instead of telling her what was really bothering him. "Lauren, I'm sorry. I—"

"I'll come back and talk to Eloise another time." Lauren fished her car keys out of her purse. "I didn't come back here to do this dance with you again."

"Then why did you come here?" He took a step closer.

"The real reason."

"That, Carter, is no longer any of your business." Lauren disappeared through the back door, leaving him alone with a whole lot of questions and a handful of snickerdoodles.

Chapter Two

LAUREN SAT IN the back of Scallywags, nursing a glass of wine and a growing sense of failure. She scrolled through the texts from the other partners at the marketing firm, all filled with one version or another of the same message—*you screwed up that last account; your father is working himself to death to get it back. If you want to keep your job, land a new one down there.*

Carter was right—Paradise Key didn't have the kind of marketing budget McNally and Webster usually wanted. Her father's firm went after the big fish, the global names: Marriott, Coca-Cola, Reebok. And if she'd been half the marketing executive her father had groomed her to be, she'd be working on an account like that.

But she wasn't. She'd never loved the business like he did, nor had she put in the hours any of her colleagues did. She had a job there because her last name was Webster, plain and simple. And if she wanted to stay, she needed to prove she could land an account, then another, and another. She'd been on the verge of leaving, of imagining something else with her life when—

Her father needed her, plain and simple. And after she'd

screwed up the account with Greyhound, her position at the company had become ten times more tenuous. She'd had, as the saying went, one job, and she'd screwed it up.

Because the passion hadn't been there. Because she hadn't cared like she should have.

In the end, she had cost the company their biggest client, a mistake the firm was just now beginning to rebound from financially. Frankly, she was lucky she hadn't been fired. The other partners said it was only because of her father that she was still there. Now the tether to her job was unwinding more with each passing day that she spent without bringing in new revenue. She'd told her father she could handle this, thinking maybe she'd find the passion for this field by starting with a client she was already familiar with—the town where she had some of her best memories. Her father was counting on her to step up and be a true part of the company. He'd leaned on her a thousand times in the years since her mother died, and Lauren couldn't let him down, not again.

Too much was on the line for her to give up now. Or to walk away just because it meant interacting with Carter again.

She signaled for a refill. The female bartender gave her a nod, then slid a beer down the bar to a rotund man who'd had four since Lauren arrived. If the man had any kind of problems like she did, she didn't fault him for wanting to bury the stress under a heavy blanket of alcohol. A minute later, the bartender delivered another drink to Lauren. "Here you go, honey. One of those nights?"

"More like one of those years, but yeah."

The other woman was a buxom redhead with a wide smile and friendly eyes. She tapped the table beside the wine. "This one's on the house. You need anything else, my name is Delilah. And honey, I hope it all gets better soon." Delilah gave her another smile and went back to the bar.

Lauren raised her glass. *Here's to me, the colossal failure.* She took a sip of wine, then sat back against the red pleather booth. Graduated top of her class, both in high school and college. Working at one of the largest marketing agencies in New York. Should have made partner at thirty—

But in the last couple of years, the wheels had come off Lauren's perfect, predictable life. Her short-lived marriage fell apart, but she'd ignored the breakup, the divorce, the empty half of the apartment for a year and a half. Then, on the morning of what would have been her second anniversary, she'd woken up alone and adrift. Lauren Webster, who achieved everything she set her mind to, was divorced and living a half life in an apartment that cost more than some people made in a lifetime and working a job she despised. She'd had that moment of thinking *is this all there is*, left her father a voicemail that she needed a vacation, and she'd done what she already had once before—escaped. One week in Vermont with her phone off had cost her the Greyhound campaign. And more.

Across from her, the dance floor sat empty. For a second, she imagined Carter walking in, pausing by her table, and putting out his hand, asking her to dance. He'd done that once, on the beach after midnight while listening to music he had on his phone. They'd laughed and danced, then tumbled to the sand and kissed under the moon. That summer seemed so far away, almost as if it had never happened.

She shook off the thoughts. Seeing him had opened a corner of her mind she normally kept sealed. Carter was her past. Right now, Lauren was focused entirely on her present.

An older couple who had been sitting in one of the booths paid their bill, then headed out after a friendly goodbye to the bartender. They paused a second while Delilah asked about their grandson, and they wished her pregnant sister well. This was Scallywags—not too busy but still loved by the locals.

Such a different world from New York. Hell, from the uppity Connecticut town where she'd grown up. Her father had never loved Paradise Key. He'd only came here for an annual vacation because Lauren's aunt lived in town, and she'd spent most of the summers teaching her niece foreign languages like German and French. Her father didn't believe in vacations unless they came with opportunities to develop an edge over the competition or steal business from the competition.

That summer, her father had stayed in New York for all of June and part of July. Her aunt had been dating a new guy, and the strict ties on Lauren's life had been loosened a little. She'd met Carter, and then spent that summer rebelling against rules and expectations. By the time her father arrived to set his daughter straight, she'd become convinced she couldn't be happy unless she was with Carter.

Then Carter had broken up with her, and the pretty little dream life she'd imagined had disappeared. She'd gone crawling back to her father, vowing to never let him down again. She'd buried herself in school and work, because there she could forget Paradise Key and Carter and the summer she almost threw her life away for someone who hadn't really loved her after all.

Now letting her hair down became something she only did to get it highlighted. Her to-do list stretched a mile long, and even these few days for Lily's funeral were five more than Lauren could spare. It would be nice to catch up with the girls, land the account, then get back to New York and find her routine, her normal, and a way to help her father and the company. Right now, he was depending on her more than ever. Then she'd stop thinking about *what-ifs* just because Carter smiled at her.

Evie came in the bar first. Tall, impossibly thin, blond, and beautiful to the point of breathtaking. She was the oldest of the group by a few months, and a talk show host on a big network in Pennsylvania. Her gaze landed on Lauren. "Hey there, stranger!" Evie put out her arms for a hug. "God, I'm so glad to see you!"

"Same here." It was like they were teenagers again the second any of them got together. She'd missed those summers and these girls. They did their best to keep in contact with phone calls, emails, and frequent texts, but it wasn't the same. Their lives had diverged after high school. Seeing each other now was a very rare occurrence. "I wish it was under different circumstances, though."

Evie's blue-gray eyes filled. "We all miss her. Such a terrible thing to lose Lily."

"It won't be the same around here." Lauren looked around the bar, thinking of the faces she knew from her past. The summers she had spent here. The moments with Carter—

Whoa. Why did her mind keep going back down that path? Had to be being back here and combining alcohol with nostalgia. She didn't need to be thinking about him in any other way than circumventing him to talk to Eloise. When Lauren had tried to talk to the tourism board member after the cookies, Eloise said she would defer to Carter's judgment. In some alternate universe of Paradise Key, Carter had become the unofficial town leader.

"Hey, two of the five best people in the world!" Sofia strode across the bar, looking amazing with her long dark hair, dark eyes, and the beauty mark above her mouth that made her stand out even more among other women. She hugged Evie, then Lauren, before the three of them settled at the table.

A round of drinks later, Jenna came in. Sofia jumped up with another hug. "She made it! Wait—you came alone?"

Jenna laughed. "Gee, I'm happy to see you all, too." She thanked Delilah for the soda the bartender handed her, then sat down with the rest of the girls.

"You know we love you, sweetheart," Evie said. "We're just dying to meet this new Romeo of yours."

Lauren took another sip of wine. She'd nearly finished glass number two, and that was making her forget about her job, her run-in with Carter, and the whole crappy event that had brought the girls back together. After enough alcohol, maybe it would just sound like a normal summer get-together. "All these stories you've told us about him make the guy sound nearly too good to be true."

Maybe it was Lauren's imagination, but Jenna sure looked uncomfortable for a second. They'd been talking in their group chat for months about Jenna's Mr. Right, and Lauren had to admit she'd felt a spark of jealousy. Not that she needed a man, especially after the fiasco her marriage and divorce had been. No, the last thing she needed—for sure— was a man in her life.

"You finally gonna spill about his name, or do we really have to keep calling him Mr. Kayak?" Evie asked.

Jenna started talking about some guy named Zach, then about her shop, and Lauren's mind drifted. Her friends seemed to have their lives together—not perfect, but more together than Lauren's mess. If only she hadn't screwed up that campaign. If only she hadn't gone to Vermont. The television spot she'd overseen had run while she was gone—but with the rough-cut, not the finished version she'd been in charge of getting to the network. And the print ad had a typo in the first line, something that normally never would have gotten past Lauren. On top of a dozen smaller mistakes with other clients, the partners had made it clear they wanted Lauren out.

But the truth was she had already lost her drive to succeed, her thirst to be the best before she even left for Vermont. During those days at the quiet inn in the woods, she'd decided she hated her job and she was going to quit.

As soon as she got back to New York, she'd told her father she was thinking of quitting. She'd seen the disappointment in his face, an echo of the look he'd given her that summer when she'd told him she was running off to be with Carter. *You're going to throw away a private school education? Going to Harvard? All the things you have worked so hard for... for some beach bum? You're worth more than that, Lauren. It's just you and me. Don't do this to me. To our family.*

She'd heard the same words in his voice that day in his office, too. But this time, they'd been weighted by a new reality—her father told her she couldn't quit. That he needed her.

Those were words Lauren had never heard before. *I need you, Lauren. The company needs you. Don't leave.*

Gerald Webster had lung cancer. And the only one he

trusted to run his company was his daughter. The one he had groomed since birth for the position.

For most of her life, it had been Lauren and her father. Her mother had died when she was nine, and she'd become the one her father put all his hopes and expectations on. Now, he was counting on her to restore the company to where it had once been, so that he could leave his legacy in capable hands. *Make me proud*, he'd said. *Make all this work worth it. I don't want to die and think I left nothing behind.*

Paradise Key wasn't Greyhound. It wasn't even Greyhound's lesser second cousin. But it was what the partners would accept as a way of keeping Lauren on, and allow her to begin to prove herself able of someday taking the reins.

Lauren sipped her wine and listened to her friends talk. The conversation circled around the table, each of them catching up in person for what they missed online before rounding back to Lauren.

"So, how's the city?" Sofia asked. "I love Key West, and the easy life with the B&B, but there are days when I imagine running off to some city and disappearing for a day or two." She laughed. "You know my family. Lots of love to go around—sometimes too much."

Lauren wanted to say no, she didn't know. Her mom was dead, and the only time she had a conversation with her father was at work. That left Lauren pretty much alone. In a city filled with millions of people. Ironic.

"Hey, you okay?" Evie nudged Lauren's shoulder. "You

sorta zoned out there."

"Yeah, yeah, fine." She fiddled with her wineglass. The other women watched and waited. Evie arched a brow.

That was the problem with reuniting with old friends. They knew her too well and knew when she was lying.

"Okay, so I kinda screwed up my job. But I've got a plan to get back on top. As long as Carter Malone doesn't get in my way."

"Carter? *The* Carter from that summer? The one you got all gaga about?"

"I did not." Lauren shook her head and laughed. "Okay, maybe I did. But he totally forgot about me after that summer, and now..."

"Now you've just realized he's still here in town and hot as hell?" Jenna grinned. "What? I live here. I see him all the time. A legally blind woman standing on Mars could tell that man was hot."

Jenna had a point. Carter *was* hot. Didn't make him a man she wanted to date again. Maybe just...sleep with. Except she wasn't the kind of woman who just slept with men, and she had more important reasons for being in this town. "Hot doesn't mean reliable or right for me. Besides, I live in New York. What's the point?"

"A hot summer fling? Sort of like before?" Evie arched a brow. "Especially since you're single now. Divorcee looking for a good time?"

Lauren scoffed. "The problem with summer flings is they

burn out as fast as they start. They have a time limit. It's in the definition."

Jenna rolled her eyes. "Come on, Lauren, live a little. At least while you're here. This is Paradise Key, remember? Make some memories."

That was what had gotten her into trouble in the first place. Not gonna go down that road twice. Lauren put some cash on her tab, then got to her feet. "Well, on that note, I better get some sleep. I'm not twenty-one anymore. Making memories requires more than two hours of sleep a night."

The girls exchanged hugs, each one tighter than the one before, narrowing the distance created by years apart. Everyone had danced around the subject of Lily and the funeral, as if speaking of it aloud made it real. But there were tears in their eyes, and the spirit of their late friend seemed to hang in the air between their hugs.

A few minutes later, Lauren stepped out into the night air, amazed at how dark it got in a place that actually did sleep, and headed to her room at a little Airbnb near the old Paradise Key Resort. Just as she pulled into the drive, her phone buzzed.

Hey, it's Carter, the text said. *Got your number from Jenna. Hope you don't mind. Can we meet for dinner tomorrow and talk? Just talk.*

Just talk? Over dinner? Sure sounded a lot more like a date than a meeting. And what did they have to talk about? Old times? Why he'd broken up with her and broken her heart? How stupid she'd been to think a summer love could be something more?

She was about to say no, then rethought her answer. Carter had an in with the tourism board. Clearly Eloise deferred to him for pretty much everything. Meeting with him could be a way for her to plead her case and help him understand what a tourism boom could do for Paradise Key. Which in turn would sway Eloise, Merle, and the town commissioners. And if she could land this account, handle it on her own, she could land another, and another, to earn the respect of the other people in the firm. So that when the time came—*if* it came—she could step into her father's shoes.

If there was one thing she'd learned from her father about marketing, it was that the pitch made all the difference. A good pitch could sell ice to Eskimos, as the cliché went. If she had just the right pitch, she could sell her plan to Carter, and he could fill Merle in, should he ever wake from his nap.

Sure, Lauren replied to the text. She even added a smiley face. No harm in making the enemy think she was on his side before she attacked. Or even better, outflanking him when he least expected it. After that summer, Carter owed her this much.

CARTER PRESSED THE cash button on the register, and the

drawer opened with a happy *ding*. He counted out two dollars and seventy-three cents, then handed the change to Mrs. Presley. "Here you are, ma'am."

She beamed up at him. "You're such a good boy, Carter. Your father must be very proud."

Mrs. Presley shopped at Malone's Market every Wednesday, and said some variation of that statement every single time she saw Carter. He did what he always did, smiled and thanked her, then carried her groceries to her car. He followed her outside, balanced the bag in one hand while he opened the passenger's side door, and then tucked the bag against the seat. "You have a good day, Mrs. Presley."

The elderly woman gave him another smile, then pressed a dollar into his palm. He'd tried at least seventy-five times to refuse the tip, but she always insisted. "Thank you, dear. See you next week."

He watched her go, then ducked back into the small shop. The white wooden frame building had stood up to many a tropical storm and the relentless Florida sun for three generations. When he'd been a kid, he'd sat on the stool by the counter, sneaking red licorice from the jar until his father shooed him out the door or put him to work. As a teenager, Carter had grown to hate the store. Sweeping the porch entryway, stocking the shelves, ringing up orders—it all seemed dorky and completely uncool. He'd looked at his father and thought, *I want more from my life than this small-town store.*

As soon as he graduated, Carter had moved to Chicago, enrolling in college for finance. He'd walked between the buildings, bundled up against the blustery wind, vowing to make something of himself. To go back to Paradise Key someday and show his father there was more to life than that tiny dot on the map.

Until his father had a heart attack, and Carter had come home to help. For the first time in his life, he'd seen the store as his father did—as a home for the people who came to shop here. The locals, who loved Paradise Key with a fierceness that bordered on obsession. They welcomed the tourists and snowbirds, but also waved goodbye at the end of the season and settled into their quiet life. In this town, people supported each other, like a pseudo-family. A little crazy, sometimes nosy, but always there when needed. He'd seen that firsthand when his father was sick. Neighbor after neighbor had been by to help his mother clean, cook meals, or take a shift at the store. It was in those moments that the jaded side of Carter began to fade, and he saw Paradise Key through new eyes.

Carter used a box cutter to open the seal on the delivery of canned goods. He started stacking the peas and carrots on the shelf, turning the labels to the front and arranging them in neat rows. The bell over the door jingled again. Carter rose and turned, about to call out a greeting, when he saw who it was.

Lauren.

The severe suit had been replaced by another, this time in steel gray with a silky pink blouse. She had on black pumps, and her hair was up in a loose bun. If he hadn't known her years ago, he would have thought she was some buttoned-up lawyer type. The exact opposite of the kind of woman he wanted, and the woman he had once been half in love with.

The Lauren he remembered had a laugh that came from someplace deep inside her. She'd been fresh-faced, sunburnt, and barefoot. That Lauren had eyes that sparkled whenever she smiled. And a zest for adventure he'd never forgotten.

A part of him wanted to coax all that out of her again. But doing that would mean getting involved with her, getting close to her, and she was only here for one reason— to turn the town he loved into some kind of tourist mecca. If there was anything he'd learned in the last couple of years, it was that Paradise Key was perfect as it was.

"This store is exactly the same," she said. Her unreadable, impassive face kept him from knowing if that was a compliment or a complaint.

"Well, not exactly," he said. "We carry Nutter Butters now."

That urged a smile out of Lauren. "My favorite cookie."

He didn't tell her that he had been the one to place the order with the distributor on a day when nostalgia got the better of him. He'd been thinking of Lauren, wondering if maybe she'd vacation in Paradise Key someday and happen to wander into his store and see the cookies. Yeah, that was what he got for drinking too much at Roger Willowby's engagement party on a warm summer night so like the ones Carter remembered with Lauren.

Instead of saying any of that, he bent and grabbed a couple of cans of corn, then pushed them into place on the shelf. "Is there something I can help you find?"

"I'm not here to buy anything, Carter. I just wanted to check out the store. I heard you took it over."

"Yup." Two cans of creamed corn were set in place to the right of their unadorned cousins.

"But I thought... Well, you seemed pretty firm on moving out of town."

"I changed my mind." He stacked the last of the vegetables, then straightened and crossed to the back of the store with the empty box. If he had hoped Lauren would leave after his minimal answers, he was wrong. She trailed along, her heels clicking on the tile floor.

"Where's your dad? Does he still work here?"

Carter spun around. "Is this market research? Or genuine curiosity? Because I'm not here to give you totals of revenue dollars brought in by tourists or percentages on the uptick in business when the snowbirds descend in January."

"I...I was just asking."

"Hard to believe you when you're dressed like a congresswoman." He closed the distance between them. She inhaled, her chest rising, then falling. Her face stayed stony.

For the hundredth time, he wondered what the hell had happened to her in the intervening years. "You're in Paradise Key, Lauren. Relax. Live a little. Like you used to."

"That's exactly what I shouldn't do. I'm not here on vacation." She blew a lock of hair off her forehead. "I don't get it, Carter. Of all the people in this town, I would think you would understand the dollars and cents of improving the economy by bringing in more tourism revenue."

"Some things are more important than creating one more must-visit vacation place." He grabbed another box, sliced through the tape, then slipped past her to begin shelving cereals. He was halfway through the Frosted Flakes when Lauren spoke again.

"Are you really being this dense?"

He bristled. Was not wanting a flood of tourists being dense? Or wisely protecting what he had? "Haven't you heard the old saying, if it ain't broke, don't fix it? No one around here wants to fix this town, Lauren. They love it just as it is."

"Are you sure about that? Because I had a casual conversation with Albert Baumann, and he told me he does the taxes for a lot of the businesses in town. He said there's more than one local shop suffering from a lack of income."

True. A flicker of guilt ran through Carter. There were some businesses in town—like Zach's kayak rentals—that depended on tourist dollars. Any dip in that revenue hurt a lot of people, like a big stone being thrown into a small pond. "That'll pick up once the snowbirds descend."

"What if they could make more money all year round?" She waved at the store. "Like this place. It's dead, Carter. What are you making, a couple of hundred a day during the off-season? You could have more customers. More business. More—"

Like a door shutting on her words, an elderly man strolled into the store, doffing his hat and tucking it under one arm. "Why hello, Carter."

Carter leaned down toward Lauren's ear. "Unless I'm going blind, too, I'd say that's a customer, Lauren." He stepped out from the aisle. "Mr. Evans. How are you today?"

"Could be worse." Jacob Evans made ninety look like the new twenty. He had a bevy of women in his neighborhood who fought over the opportunity to cook dinner for him and be on his arm when he went dancing down at the VFW hall on Wednesday nights. Carter's father had known Jacob from the day he opened the store, and he often went fishing with him on Saturday afternoons when Jacob said he needed a break from the constant chattering of the women. "I need to pick up a little something for Gladys. I told her I'd bring the wine if she brought the roast chicken."

Carter chuckled. "Isn't that what Ms. Simmons made you on Sunday?"

"She did indeed. Any other man might refuse the same dinner twice in one week, but Gladys...she's got a roast chicken that will make you sing. That woman can cook."

Jacob leaned over. "And kiss. She's a firecracker, that Gladys."

Carter knew Gladys Sanderson, who called Bingo on Tuesday nights at the Presbyterian church and won best in show at the horticultural fair every year. She was in her late eighties, five feet tall, and had a shock of white hair that surrounded her head like a cloud. Firecracker wasn't the first word that came to Carter's mind, but he was glad Jacob was happy. "Well, you have a great evening, Mr. Evans." Carter slid the wine bottle into a paper bag, then took the cash to make change.

Jacob turned to Lauren. "You must be new in town," he said. "I haven't seen a woman this beautiful in Paradise Key since I was in my forties. Carter's a lucky man."

"Oh, he's not..." Lauren's face reddened. "We're not...We're just friends. Sort of."

Jacob chuckled. "There's always room in a *sort of* for something more." He thumbed toward Carter. "This one is a keeper. We're all real proud of him in this town. He does more for Paradise Key than that entire useless board of commissioners. Why, I don't know what we would have done without him last year after the hurricane hit us, or this year when Ken Gershwin's house burned down. He's a credit to his father, that's for sure."

"Here's your change, Mr. Evans," Carter said, cutting in before his matchmaking customer set up an appointment with a preacher.

Lauren's phone rang just then. She made a face, then turned to Carter. "I need to take this. We can talk later tonight."

"Okay, sure." He watched her walk out of the store, wondering if her slacks-covered legs were just as sexy as he remembered. Maybe more so with the black pumps she wore now. He imagined himself unpinning her hair and trailing kisses along her neck…

"I see you've got your own firecracker." Jacob nodded in the direction of the door Lauren had just passed through.

"Lauren? She's not…she's…well, she's an old friend."

"That's what she tried to claim, too." Jacob chuckled. "I can read women like they're billboards on the highway. And that woman is in-ter-est-ed in you." He said the last in a singsong, with another knowing nod. "Best make your move before some other rooster takes over the hen house."

"I don't know about that, Mr. Evans." Lauren clearly had *keep away* written all over her. He doubted another man was going to have any luck making a move. And yet, a part of him had a flash of jealousy at the thought. "But we do have dinner plans tonight," he said, then wondered why he was telling Jacob any of this.

"If you want my advice…" Jacob leaned over the counter and lowered his voice. "There are three things you can't do enough with a woman. Tell her she's beautiful, treat her like a lady, and kiss her goodnight."

Carter doubted he would do any of the above. Their

meeting was business. Strictly business. His whole intent in asking her to dinner was to find a quiet place where he could persuade her to leave well enough alone when it came to Paradise Key. But then he thought of the sight of Lauren as she walked out the door, and knew he was fooling himself.

Chapter Three

I T WAS JUST a business meeting, Lauren told herself as she tried on her third outfit of the evening. It didn't matter what she wore. Carter wasn't interested in her that way, and she definitely wasn't interested in him. At all.

But as she stood in front of the mirror of her room, which was housed in a four-bedroom converted into a rental property for vacationers, she knew better. Just being in this town reminded her of that summer with Carter. All those long, hot nights when she had snuck out of the resort to meet him by the pier. The night world had seemed so desolate, so *theirs*, with the miles of empty beach and the quiet hush of the lapping waves. They would sit on the cool sand and talk for hours while the water tickled their toes and the stars glinted off the ocean.

She'd run away that summer, literally and figuratively. She'd gotten swept up in the tropical location, the headiness of a temporary love, and almost thrown away her life for a man who didn't want her. Lauren no longer put stock in foolish ideas about love. The best marriage, she had decided long ago, would be one between two equals who could share conversations over the Sunday paper, without any of that crazy headiness that made for some very bad decisions. That was what her parents had been like, from what she could remember. Her father often said he'd never remarry because he had never found someone who was as compatible with him as her mother had been. He never talked of those days like a man in love, or a man who had lost his other half. It had all been practical and content, he'd often said. A marriage of equals.

That was what her marriage had been. Her ex also worked in marketing, and it had made sense on paper to marry him. They spoke the same work language, liked the same movies, and enjoyed the same kinds of food.

And had absolutely zero chemistry. She could have married her brother for all the attraction she had to her ex-husband. Whereas with Carter...

Hot wasn't an adequate adjective for that summer. Explosive. Unforgettable. Achingly amazing—

And utterly painful at the end. That was the part she needed to remember—how a wild ride like that could end. Far better to find another quiet, predictable relationship someday.

Her father had called her this afternoon, just a quick status report call, but one that reminded Lauren her priority was the company, not Carter. As with pretty much everything in life, her father didn't bother with pleasantries or trite conversations. He hadn't wanted to hear about the weather in Paradise Key or the temperature of the water.

He'd asked a simple, *did you land the account yet?* When she answered in the negative, he'd said, *I expected more of you.* Then he hung up, and she'd been left feeling like she had failed. Again. He hadn't spoken of his health or latest doctor appointment—two other personal conversational areas her father rarely ventured into. Knowing Gerald Webster, he was avoiding the topic so he wouldn't have to face reality.

In the end, Lauren opted for an unfussy dark blue dress and a pair of kitten heels. She put her hair back with a barrette, and kept her makeup light. The mirror reflected serious but not buttoned-up. *Like a congresswoman.*

Did Carter really see her like that? All business, no pleasure?

And why the hell did she care? She needed this account, then she'd be on the first plane back to New York. Back to her father, to making sure he took it easy and stopped worrying about the future of McNally and Webster.

She grabbed her purse before heading out of the room without a second glance in the mirror. The drive across town to Lombardi's didn't take long. The sun had gone down, and most folks were in for the evening. The night air was warm, the sky clear and peppered with stars. Lauren parked in the lot, then headed into the restaurant.

Soft jazz music played over the sound system, the perfect undertow to the soft murmur of voices. The Italian restaurant had an Old European feel to it, with dark furniture and a thick crimson carpet. She caught the scent of lasagna and eggplant parmigiana as a waiter walked by, a full tray balanced on one shoulder.

The hostess seated her in a booth, then handed Lauren a menu. A second later, Carter walked in. He paused by the hostess station while his eyes adjusted to the dim interior. It gave her a moment to compose herself before he reached the table.

Because he looked good. No, not just good. *Damned good.*

Carter had opted for a pale blue button-down shirt, unbuttoned at the neck. The color complemented his brown eyes and his dark brown hair. The same unruly wave curled across his brow, and a part of her itched to brush it back. A pair of dark blue trousers hugged Carter's body like they'd been made for him. Holy hell. Had he stressed about his attire like she had? Or had he just thrown something on, without a care about what she would think? Either way, he could have walked off the cover of *GQ* magazine. Lauren wasn't the only woman who watched him cross the room.

He slid into the booth. "Am I late? Or are you early?"

She laughed. "You know me. Early is my middle name. I hate to be late to anything."

"I remember. But I also remember there were times when you weren't in an all-fired rush. Times when you wanted to…take our time."

A moment ticked between them, charged with memories, with an attraction that had never died. She wondered what adult Carter would be like as a lover. Would he linger, explore every curve, be sure she had as much pleasure as he did? When they'd been young, he'd found her body an endless source of wonder. They'd spent hours simply tracing patterns on the skin of each other's back or kissing a trail from one end to the other.

It had been over a year since her divorce, two years since she'd had sex because her marriage with Jason had ended long before it was official. Maybe she was just lonely, and that made Carter seem twice as tempting. Yeah, that was it.

Liar.

"Well, um…" She cleared her throat and picked up her menu to block her face, along with the blush surely blooming in her cheeks. "What's good here?"

"Pretty much everything. They hand-make the pasta and sauce. I can tell you from experience that the lasagna is to die for."

She skimmed the offerings, avoiding Carter's eyes. "Have you been here a lot?"

"A fair amount. Enough to know I love the lasagna, I'm not a big fan of the spinach ravioli, and I might name my first child after the panna cotta."

She peeked over the top of the menu. "That good?"

He grinned. "Let's just say they know to bring me a dish of it every time I come here."

Every time. Had he been here a lot? With other women? On dates? She ducked behind her menu wall again. "Does your girlfriend like the panna cotta too?"

Was that obvious fishing? Or would he see it as small talk? And why was she asking, anyway? Hadn't she just been thinking she didn't need a man in her life?

"I don't have a girlfriend, Lauren," Carter said. "In case you were wondering."

Busted. "Oh, well, okay."

"What about you? Is there some guy waiting for you back in New York?"

She scoffed and set the menu aside. "I work so much I barely have time to water my plants, never mind date. I'm on my third ficus in a year, and I finally gave up on the spider plant two months ago. And the ex-husband walked out two years ago."

"You killed a spider plant? Isn't that one of the easiest to grow? I'm not even going to ask about the ex-husband." Carter grinned. "I assume he's still alive?"

"Last I heard, yes, he's alive." She laughed. "I can feed myself, and on occasion, another human being. But plants, well…" Lauren shrugged. "They don't fare so well at my house."

"Well, hell. I'm glad I'm not a cactus."

That made her laugh, but also had her wondering if he'd meant more than a joke by his words. Before she could decide, the waitress came by. Lauren ordered a glass of chardonnay to ease her nerves, and the recommended lasagna. Carter opted for a beer and the same dinner.

"Before you criticize my gardening skills, how many plants do you have in your house, Mr. Green Thumb?" Lauren asked after the waitress left.

"Well, none. But I'm not exactly a houseplant kind of guy. That was…" He shook his head. "Anyway, we're not here to talk about our pasts."

"No. Of course not." Though she still wasn't sure what they were going to talk about, or what had been left in the words that trailed off. Seemed they'd covered everything earlier at the store. When she'd impulsively popped into Malone's Market, she'd thought she could catch Carter off guard, make him see the importance of increasing business. Instead, the conversation had ended the same way their last one had—two dogs sitting on opposite ends of the same bone.

She needed a new tactic. A new argument. Except right now, watching the fine muscles of his hands as he drummed his fingers on the table, all she could think about was what it would feel like to be touched by Carter again.

What had he been leaving out when he'd said *that was…* and then changed the subject? Was it whatever caused the shadows in his eyes? Asking would be getting personal, and if there was one thing she'd learned in working with clients, it was that getting personal only muddied everything.

"Let's talk about the present," she said. "Like why you're running your dad's store instead of being CFO for some international multi-billion-dollar company."

Apparently, her new tactic was direct and nosy questions.

"I did work at an international multi-billion-dollar company," Carter said. "Made more money than I could spend in a year. Even had a nice little corner office and a company car."

She could imagine him like that. Suit and tie—just the thought made her pulse race—commanding a room, leading a team. Carter had a way of carrying himself that said he could tame any situation, handle any crisis. Even when they were young, she'd loved his calm, quiet steadiness the most. He'd been such an antidote to her father's constant stress, high expectations, and the stuffy life she led in Connecticut.

It was little wonder that with him, she'd been unafraid to take risks. It was as if his calmness had made her braver, happier. She'd become someone else that summer, someone who didn't have to follow the stringent rules her father exacted, someone who didn't care about grades or futures or anything outside of the little world she had created with Carter.

It had all been a fantasy, of course, a temporary honeymoon from her real life. Carter had broken up with her at the end of the summer, she'd gone back to Connecticut, and those months with him in Paradise Key faded in her memory.

Mostly.

The waitress returned. Carter accepted his drink, thanked the waitress, then raised his glass toward Lauren's.

"Cheers. To old friends."

She clinked with him, then took a long sip of the chardonnay. Nice and dry with hints of oak and pear. "Is that what we are? Friends?"

"What we are, my dear Lauren, is complicated."

My dear Lauren. The words fluttered inside her. He hadn't meant anything by them, she was sure, but still... "Complicated sounds about right."

He fiddled with his glass for a minute. The sound system played softly, while a table of ten left the restaurant in a noisy rush of kids and chatty adults. When the room settled down again, Carter spoke. "I was happy working at the firm in Chicago. Hated the winters, compared to the weather here, but I loved what I did. I figured I'd be doing that the rest of my life, just like I'd always dreamed. I had, like I told you, the American dream. Even had a fiancée and an entire life planned. Then my father had a heart attack."

"Oh, I'm so sorry, Carter. I had no idea." She had only met Carter's father a few times. Roger Malone was one of those affable guys who knew everyone in town, remembered their name and their kids' names, and made shopping in his store feel like old home week. Carter and his father had a difficult relationship, or at least they had the summer she'd dated him. His father wanted him to work more in the store, and Carter just wanted to be an unencumbered teenager. They'd clashed often when they worked together from what Lauren remembered. "Is he okay now?"

Carter nodded. "I flew home right after it happened. Just to help my mom out, you know? She's getting into her sixties. Running the store and taking care of my dad put a lot on her shoulders. I figured I'd be here a week, two tops." He put his hands out. "Still here, three years later."

"Three years? Wow. That's a long time." She glanced at his hand, but didn't see a ring. Had the fiancée stayed in Chicago? Was she part of the *that was...*?

He nodded. "I'm pretty sure they cleaned out my office at the old job. That's okay. The view is better here."

She wondered for a second if he meant the view across the table. Then she checked herself, and went back to the topic at hand. What had driven Carter to come back to this town, and how could she use those emotions to sway him into her camp? That was easier than thinking about why it bothered her that he'd come back here and settled down in the very place he told her he wanted to leave—the fundamental reason behind their breakup. *There's no sense keeping in touch. I'm leaving this town the first chance I get, and I don't want my life to be tied down when I do.*

Except he had almost married someone else. What had she had that Lauren didn't? And why was she even giving that space in her mind? She cleared her throat, pushing those thoughts out of her head. "Do you ever think about going back into corporate finance?"

Carter took a long sip of beer. "Sometimes. I'm not going to lie; the money is fabulous. I'm driving a used Jeep now instead of a Mercedes. And my Armani suits are just gathering dust in the closet. But I've grown to really love the kind of life here."

"What kind of life is that?" Carter had been the one who said Paradise Key was a certain kind of hell. He'd talked often about wanting to leave, to see the world. Now he saw it as a good place to settle down?

Back then, she'd been the one trying to sell him on staying in Paradise Key. She'd looked at the town as a respite from the demanding life she'd led. The expectations she hated. She'd lain awake at night, picturing herself and Carter living in a cottage by the beach, far from the reach of her father and the future he had designed for her. Back when she was a teenager, the summers here had felt like the only time she could truly *be*. Turned out those were the foolish dreams of a foolish teenage girl.

Although, hadn't she recaptured that feeling of respite when she was on the beach the other day? All alone, listening to the ocean's song, watching the seagulls dive for their lunch? Real life, though, didn't exist in some cottage on the beach with a boy who'd only loved her until the end of August. Real life came with bills and rent and a sick father who was expecting her to become the daughter she should have been all along. *Someday this company will be yours,* her father often said, with the unspoken message that he expected her to not only carry on his legacy, but also make it even bigger. The trouble? Lauren didn't love the job her father lived for.

Surely Carter could relate to that. He'd returned to town to help his own father. He, of all people, would understand why she would be committed to doing the same.

"Trust me, I'm just as surprised as you are that I changed my mind about Paradise Key," Carter said, drawing her attention back to the conversation. "I always thought it was boring, dull, and predictable. But that, ironically, is what creates the environment I love. And what makes it so special to my father, too."

Except for that snippet of time on the beach the other day, she couldn't remember the last time she'd felt calm or peaceful. The last time she'd had room to breathe, a space to forget about her problems. Yes, she could—that summer before her freshman year of college. Right now, it seemed a million years in the past. "How so?"

"You didn't have a chance to get to know my father that summer. Honestly, I never really did, either, not until I moved back here and started working in the store."

"I can understand that. I've spent more time with my father at work than anywhere else." The worry she felt about her father was one more thing she had in common with this new adult Carter.

"It's been great for our relationship," Carter said. "And a way for me to find out more about him, things I never knew before. I'd been working at the store for a week when these two elderly women came in. The Michaels sisters. They're not twins, but they look like they could be. They've lived together in a little house on First Street their entire lives. Happy spinsters, they call themselves." He chuckled. "Anyway, they came in one day, and bought some PVC pipe and a pipe wrench. They paid, I put it in a bag, and Sarah, the younger sister, took the bag and handed it right back to me. 'Dinner will be at six,' she said. 'You might need some of that purple glue stuff.'"

Lauren cocked her head to one side. "Dinner?"

"I stared at her, thinking she'd lost her mind. Her older sister Emma piped up and said, 'Your father will know what we mean.' Sure enough, my father had been doing repairs and odd jobs for Emma and Sarah for years. I went over there, fixed a broken drain pipe under the kitchen sink, then had meatloaf and mashed potatoes and heard at least a dozen stories about my dad."

"That must have been really nice."

"It was. I saw a whole other side of him. You know my dad—friendly as hell, but not the most emotional guy. He'd give you the shirt off his back, but when it comes to talking about himself, he usually goes mute. I never knew my father rescued a little boy who almost drowned, or that he'd once sat in at tree for an hour to convince Mrs. Presley's tiger cat to climb down. That he had delivered medicine in a hurricane, and then fed a hundred people out of his own pocket after the storm."

"He did?"

Carter nodded. "I asked my mom why she never told me, and she said my father is a humble man. He doesn't want people making a big deal out of things we all should do without a second thought. My father believes we are put here to help each other, and so he does that in spades every day of his life. He's made me want to be a better man. Someone who does more than just shows up at work every day."

"Wow. That's really awesome. I don't see a lot of that in New York City." Or meet a lot of men who said what Carter had. She'd thought he was intriguing at eighteen. He was damned near intoxicating now.

"I bet. I didn't see much in Chicago, either, but I see a lot of that giving spirit here. Paradise Key is a world unto itself, Lauren. That's what I'm trying to explain."

"Even a world unto itself needs to bring in revenue, Carter. Florida is a tourism state, not a manufacturing one. The entire state depends on tourists to pay the bills."

"I get that. I do. And I'm not trying to cut the tourism money we already bring in," he said. "But I also don't want to turn this place into another destination for an episode of *MTV Gone Wild*."

She scoffed. "That's a big reach for one marketing campaign, and not what I had in mind."

"I've seen some of the other campaigns your company has designed," he said. "They aren't exactly in keeping with the spirit I'd like to bring to Paradise Key."

"My father is a big believer in going all out." Lauren

knew the advertising slogans Carter was referring to. Controversial, hard-hitting, shocking—those were the words that described Gerald's approach to marketing. Lauren had disagreed with many of the tactics, which had put her at odds with her father more than once. "A lot of what you see McNally and Webster produce is his, not mine. I'm more...conservative in my approach. Too conservative, if you ask my father."

All her life, Lauren had struggled with living up to what her father expected of her. What he thought she was capable of, how he wanted her to step into his shoes. And almost every time, she fell short.

Now, the stakes were higher. Her father was sick, and that meant she needed to stop dreaming about what could have been and step into the role she'd been groomed for since birth. Starting with landing Paradise Key to make up a tiny bit of what it cost them in losing Greyhound, and begin to establish her worth at McNally and Webster.

"Conservative can be good." Carter sipped his wine. "We worked with an agency many years ago that was the opposite of conservative. I think that's a big part of what makes the town reluctant to try another company. Plus, we've been getting by pretty well, just relying on word of mouth."

"I can design something that works to fit the McNally and Webster approach, yet also fits the town," Lauren said. "Just let me get in front of the tourism board—"

A different waitress delivered their lasagna, interrupting

the conversation. This one was a thin brunette with a tiny waist and a big chest, who leaned in Carter's direction just a bit too much. "Nice to see you in here again, Carter," she said.

"Uh, thanks, Heidi." He cleared his throat, and averted his gaze from the shelf of breasts close to his face. The waitress dropped Lauren's plate on the table with attitude, then stormed off, clearly annoyed at the unreciprocated flirting.

Not that Lauren cared whether Carter had a dating history with some huffy waitress. Or a fiancée he hadn't mentioned again. He was a handsome man—of course he'd date. Some other woman would undoubtedly see him as a keeper, like the customer in the store had mentioned earlier. Then why did it take a second to redirect her thoughts? Why did she watch Carter, hoping he didn't cast a look in Heidi's direction?

He kept his attention on Lauren's face. He was either very interested in the conversation or very smart. "What makes you so protective of this town?" Lauren asked. She fiddled with her fork instead of eating, telling herself she didn't care about Heidi, only about the reason she was here. "A thousand other people wouldn't care as much as you do."

"It's hard to put into words, Lauren. When I worked in Chicago, I handled millions of dollars at a time. I had massive responsibilities, dozens of employees working under me. It was all I'd ever dreamed of, but I wasn't happy. I came home to run this store while my father got back on his feet, and in one evening over meatloaf, I found something I didn't even know I was missing."

"What's that?"

"Pride. In my father. In this town. In myself. My father had set an example, and all I wanted to do was live up to it. Not just running the store, but helping the town in as many ways as I can, like with the tourism board. I don't know if I'm half the man my father was, but I'm trying."

Lauren hadn't even realized she'd been leaning forward, caught up in his words, until she went to reach for her wineglass. Pride. When was the last time she had felt a swell of that in her chest? Most days, her job kept her too busy to have lunch, never mind notice a feeling. She had worked countless late nights, endless weekends, early mornings. Even her dreams were filled with work, especially when the office was under a noose-tight deadline. But she could relate to the idea of taking what his father had made and making it more. That was what Lauren was trying to do, too. Not because she wanted it, but because her father needed it. "That's…that's awesome, Carter."

"I want to be the kind of man my father has been. I want to take care of this town, these people, the way he has. And that," he raised his wineglass in her direction, "is why I am so protective of Paradise Key."

Wow. If Carter had been in advertising, he could have sold her the Brooklyn Bridge with that speech. How was she going to argue with that? How could she ask him to do her this favor of getting this small, homespun, baking-apple-pies-for-the-neighbor town to agree to a major marketing push? If anything, this conversation had made her job harder because she felt like a heel for even thinking about using his connections.

Except she was doing this for the same reasons. She wanted her father to be proud of her, to show him that she could do this on her own, that he could count on her. To repay him for what her lack of enthusiasm and mistakes had cost the company, a company he had poured his entire life into. There was no time to come up with another plan, to finesse another client, to land another account. She had foolishly put all her eggs in this one basket, thinking her history with the town and the people who remembered her would be enough.

She'd told her father the morning she left for Paradise Key that the deal was as good as signed. There was no way she wanted to go back there and disappoint him again.

She'd been overly confident. Fact was, she hadn't been here for a vacation in a decade. Those connections had moved away or died, and the town was not as eager for her help as she had expected. All in all, a foolish plan, but right now, it was the only one she had. No one at McNally and Webster trusted her to handle their clients, and she knew she had to do this alone, or she'd never earn the respect of her coworkers. Never show her father that she could carry on his legacy.

Lauren finally took a bite of her dinner. "This is amazing. You were right." The lasagna was exactly as promised, steamy, cheesy, and the perfect interruption to the conversation. As they ate, the conversation shifted to the food, then the updates she had about Sofia, Evie, and Jenna. It was an easy back and forth, full of small talk and a few shared memories.

Carter had been right. The lasagna was incredible. The panna cotta even more so. And a great reason to focus on something other than the impossible situation she found herself in now.

"I'm glad your dad is doing okay now," Lauren said. "I know firsthand how scary that can be."

"Firsthand?" Carter pushed his empty plate to the side. "Is your dad okay?"

She started to brush the question off with a vague *he's fine*, but then the tears welled in her eyes and her voice got thick, and all she could say was, "He's sick."

"Sick?" Carter reached out and took her hand. "Lauren, I'm so sorry. Is he going to be all right?"

She bit her lip and shrugged, if only to keep the tears from spilling over. She hadn't realized until just that second how worried and scared she was about her father's health. "He's got the best doctors, of course. And hopefully he's listening to them. He quit smoking, so that's something."

"If you need anything, even if it's just someone to vent

to, let me help."

Damn Carter for being so nice. Helpful. She wanted to hate him, she truly did, but she couldn't. "Thank you."

Their original waitress came by with the check. The interruption gave Lauren a second to compose herself and swallow back her tears. Carter seemed to sense she didn't want to talk about it anymore, because as soon as the waitress left, he changed the subject.

"So, what about you?" he asked as he laid a credit card on the bill before she could offer to split it. "That summer you were here, you talked about wanting to experience life. To go skiing and traveling and climbing mountains. Or at least do some more paddleboarding."

Being around Carter had been like escaping prison. They'd snuck out at night, gone skinny-dipping, snuck beers in the afternoon—essentially all the things normal teenagers did—but Lauren never had. Every day with Carter had been an adventure, and toward the end of the summer, she'd begun to think about a future. About running away, staying in Paradise Key, and spending every night under the stars in his arms.

Then he had told her their relationship had an expiration date. That as soon as his senior year was over, he was off to a life far from Paradise Key. Far from her.

"No. I grew up and got practical. Everyone has one crazy summer, don't they?" she said. "To get it out of their system."

"So no mountains or paddleboards?" he asked.

She shrugged. "I have rent to pay. Responsibilities at work. I can't just run off and spend the day on the water." Although she was sure that was exactly the kind of thing Jenna would go and do with Zach, her kayak guy. Jenna sounded so happy when she talked about Zach. Once upon a time, Lauren had thought she could have that kind of happiness, too, but—

No point dwelling on things she no longer believed in. She was here for her job, not some kind of happily-ever-after fantasy.

"That is exactly what I think you should do." Carter signed the receipt, then handed it to the waitress and tucked his credit card away. "Take the day off tomorrow and spend it with me. I'm sure I can get my dad to cover my shift at the store so we can go have fun. Like we used to."

The idea tempted her. It would be like reliving a little of that summer. That wonderful, painful, incredible summer.

She got to her feet, then grabbed her purse. "Thank you for dinner. You really didn't have to pay. We talked business. You should have let me cover it."

"You can. Tomorrow." He grinned. "After we go paddleboarding."

"You're awfully insistent on this." *For someone who pretends he isn't interested in me anymore. For someone who let me go without a second thought.*

"What's so wrong with a little fun, Lauren? I'm sure

you've been stressed about work, your dad, and losing Lily. It's okay to take some time for yourself."

She didn't answer him. Damn Carter for being right, and for making the idea so tempting. They walked out of the restaurant, navigating the crowded tables before stepping into the warm night air. He held the door for her. As she passed him, she had to resist the urge to draw in the dark, woodsy scent of his cologne.

She fished her keys out of her purse. "I'll see you later."

He put a hand on hers. Electricity sizzled in her veins, and all those excuses she was trying to hold tight to began to slip away. "Tomorrow. Say you'll see me tomorrow. Spend one day of your vacation with me. Like the old days."

She shook her head, trying to hide the disappointment that filled her when his touch dropped away. "I'm here for a funeral, Carter, not fun."

He sobered. "True. But you have a few days left, right? Take a vacation. If I know you, it's been a long time since you did."

"Why do you want to do this?" She should have just said good night and left instead of arguing with him, but she couldn't seem to bring herself to unlock her car, to walk away, to let the night end. "To persuade me not to go after Paradise Key's marketing budget?"

He raised his gaze to the stars, letting out a long breath. "Why is everything about money and work with you, Lauren? When we were teenagers—"

"Which was more than a decade ago—"

His gaze returned to hers. Piercing, knowing, firm. "You told me that you never wanted to turn out like your father. A workaholic who only enjoyed his life for one week out of the year."

And even then, Lauren's father had worked on vacation, rarely spending a moment with his daughter. Yes, he was a workaholic, but he was one who was depending on her. "I shouldn't. I have—"

"One day, Lauren. That's all I ask." He grinned. "In return, I'll hear you out on your ideas for the town. Quid pro quo. If anything, think of it as me making things up to you."

"You did dump me pretty harshly." She fiddled with her keys, watching him out of the corner of her eye. What harm would it be to spend a few hours with him? And maybe, just maybe, in a relaxed environment, Carter would not only be more open to her ideas, as he'd said, but even come on board enough to convince the rest of the town. In the process, Lauren could restore her father's faith in her, and change the world.

Well, the last might be impossible, but she'd be content with the first one.

"Okay," she said finally.

His grin widened. He shifted closer to her. "Did I just hear you say yes?"

"Well, yes to one day. I mean, not even a whole day. Maybe just a few hours…"

"You still talk too much," Carter whispered. At some point, he had moved even closer until only a few millimeters separated them. "What's it going to take to get you to stop?"

Lauren huffed. "I don't talk—"

He kissed her. Leaned in and invaded her space and kissed her. Like they hadn't broken up a decade ago. Like they were still together. Like he could still affect her with a simple kiss.

Turned out, she realized as she leaned into Carter, too, almost as if she couldn't help it, he could.

Chapter Four

S WEET WINE AND bittersweet memories.

That was what Lauren Webster tasted like when Carter kissed her. He didn't know what he'd been thinking—okay, so maybe he hadn't been thinking at all—but as soon as his lips met hers, he knew this was a bad idea.

Not because kissing her was bad. Far from it. Kissing Lauren was like sliding into a cool pool on a hot day, easy and sensual and familiar. He had missed her, damn it, far more than he realized until just now.

She leaned into him, and her hands slid up his back. Carter deepened the kiss, hungry for her, hungrier than he'd been for the lasagna or the panna cotta. He knew every curve of her body. Knew she liked a kiss that eased from slow to hot, and that when she met his tempo with her own, the desire between them would ignite.

And he knew how easy it was to fall for her, and how much of a mistake that would be.

He cupped her jaw for one long moment, wanting more, wanting her, then he stepped back and broke the kiss. Her cheeks were red, her breathing fast, her eyes wide. And all he wanted to do was kiss her again.

"What was that?" she said.

"If I have to remind you…" He smirked. "You didn't pay attention in health class."

"I meant, what was that between us? We broke up, Carter. A decade ago. And we're not getting involved again. At all. Ever."

"Of course not." Except it hadn't felt like they were broken up when they were kissing. And her repeated insistence they weren't getting involved again sure sounded like the proverbial lady protesting too much.

"Then why did you kiss me?" she asked.

He didn't have an answer for that. She'd been standing under the golden pool of light from the streetlamp, her eyes bright, her lips moving, and the soft scent of her floral perfume tangling between them. He'd shifted closer, just to make room for people exiting the building he told himself, and like a magnet, the pull between them intensified. He'd stopped listening to her words, because suddenly, the desire to have her, to touch her, overpowered any rational thought.

"It won't happen again," he said. Because it was a bad idea. Though he couldn't remember why exactly.

"Well…that's good." She released her hair from the barrette and ran a hand through her hair, displacing the blond waves from straight to just tumbled out of bed.

Damn. When she did that, the desire he thought he'd quelled by ending their kiss roared to life again. And he knew he'd just lied to himself and her. He *was* going to kiss her again. Not tonight, but soon. And not once, but many, many times. Maybe then Carter could get Lauren Webster out of his system. For good.

SHE LOOKED LIKE a nun heading out for a day in the sun.

The long-sleeved shirt, capris, and wide-brimmed hat Lauren put on Friday morning screamed *not sexy*. She told herself she was protecting her skin from UV rays, but really, she was protecting her lips from another kiss. Well, protecting wasn't exactly the truth, because ever since Carter had kissed her last night, Lauren had been unable to think of anything else.

Not her job. Not her quest to land Paradise Key for a marketing campaign. Not her future or her upcoming rent payment or the price of squash in China. All night, she had tossed and turned, reliving the kiss when she was awake, then taking it to the next step in her dreams. For a second when she woke up this morning, she'd been still caught between dreams and reality and had thought Carter was next to her in the bed. She'd had a second of contentment, then the rising sun woke her the rest of the way, and she realized the other half of the bed was empty, the sheets cool.

Thank goodness.

Lauren headed into the small coffee shop in downtown Paradise Key, and picked a small round table by the window.

The space was empty, save for one elderly couple a few tables away. The place was homey, bright, and the aroma of coffee filled the air. Lauren thought of the breakfasts she and the girls had at the Paradise Key Resort when they'd all been vacationing there as teenagers. The beautiful hotel was shuttered now, worn down by the merciless Florida sun and the toll of recent hurricanes.

Jenna came striding in, and beelined for Lauren's table. They exchanged a quick hug, then Jenna sat in the opposite chair. The lone waitress immediately poured them two coffees, but Jenna waved off the menu. "No time to eat. I have to get to work in a few minutes." She turned to Lauren. "I'm glad you invited me for coffee. It seems like we never get a chance to totally catch up."

"True. It's not like those lazy summer days when all we'd do was hang out and get into trouble."

Jenna laughed. "Those days were fun, weren't they? I miss not having to be responsible for anything." She sighed. "Now I have my shop, which keeps me crazy busy."

"How did it go with the commission about your expansion?" The other night, Jenna had told Lauren and the girls she'd put in a request with Paradise Key to expand her shop. Business had been good, but she needed more space to handle the extra influx of customers.

Jenna rolled her eyes. "They move like mud over there. Took me months to get that approval, but I finally did. Zach hasn't been so lucky. He needs some road repairs and a sewer line repaired in front of his shop after that sinkhole opened. They told him two weeks. I swear, this entire town is against change."

"You can say that again." Lauren took a sip of her coffee. Strong and dark just like she drank it at home, to keep her energized for crazy long hours. In the last few days, Lauren had grown to like the lazier pace of Paradise Key life. She had to admit she didn't miss the frenetic deadline driven world she'd left behind in New York. That alone was a sign she'd been here too long, if these island breezes were lulling her into complacency. "I'm trying to get a meeting with the tourism board to talk about a marketing campaign for Paradise Key. And so far, I've only been able to talk to Carter Malone. Thanks for giving him my number, by the way."

Mischief lit Jenna's face. "Hey, just helping out a friend. Besides, he really does have sway with the tourism board, especially Eloise, who has a major crush on him and acts like he's the president of the entire country. Can't say I blame her. Carter is easy on the eyes, you know."

Oh, Lauren knew. She also knew how unforgettable the man could be—and how infuriating. When Carter wanted to be a roadblock, he put all six-plus feet of himself in the way. "Yeah, but because of him, I can't talk to Eloise or Merle or even get a meeting with Tyson Braddock, who I heard has some sway over tourism initiatives since he's on the board of commissioners."

"Paradise Key is very much about keeping things as they

are. Except for Tyson, who's a jerk but definitely wants to change things up, even if he runs into opposition with everyone else around here." Jenna chuckled. "It's part of what I love about this place and what totally drives me nuts. It's like a giant family—nosy and aggravating but in the end, protective and there for you when you need them."

Lauren waved off the offer of a refill of her coffee. "So what kept you here instead of moving away?"

Jenna fiddled with her mug. "I guess I like the routine, the predictability of small-town living. Then my grandmother needed help with the shop. Next thing I know, she's handing it over to me, and well…" She glanced at her watch. "Damn, I have to go. I need to open in a few minutes." She tossed a couple of bills on the table before getting to her feet. "Stop by the shop later if you want."

"I can't. I have…plans."

"Plans? Like what kind? Because the way you said it, it almost sounds like you have a…" Jenna leaned closer, and Lauren felt her face heat. "You have a date, don't you? With Carter? You, who insisted there was no way in hell you would have another summer fling while you were here?"

"It's not a fling. And not a date. Just…" Lauren shrugged. "Okay, so maybe it is a date. But it doesn't mean anything. I'm only doing it so I can talk to him about the marketing proposal. The man won't let me make an appointment, and insists we spend the day out on the water."

"While you admire his hot body and fantasize about

what it would be like to kiss him again?"

"Well, I kinda already did that yesterday." Lauren shook her head. "I have no idea why because I'm not normally a spontaneous person. I know better than to fall for some guy who has already dumped me once."

"You *are* spontaneous—when you're here." Jenna grinned. "There's just something about this place, isn't there? Makes you do things you wouldn't normally do."

Something in Jenna's tone told Lauren that her friend, who had just said she liked predictably and routine, had stepped outside the lines of her life. Lauren wanted to ask more, but Jenna waved goodbye and hurried out of the coffee shop.

A few minutes later, Lauren had paid her bill. She stepped onto the wide verandah that faced the street. From here, she could see Jenna's shop and her apartment just above it on 2nd Street. Jenna was just turning the sign to read OPEN and sent a wave Lauren's way.

Lauren waved back, trying not to pace the planked floor. Carter would be here any second to pick her up, and she had yet to develop a game plan for today. She'd spent more time worrying about what she was going to wear than how she was going to sell him a marketing campaign idea he could get behind.

The main number for McNally and Webster lit up her phone. Lauren drew in a deep breath, then answered. "Hi, Dad."

"Where's that new account?" The booming voice of her father echoed through the earpiece. "You told me to give you a chance, to prove you had the chops to be a valuable part of this company. This should be a walk in the park with the McNally and Webster name behind you. I heard that new marketing firm in SoHo landed a sweet deal with the city of Tampa. A firm in *SoHo,* Lauren. A tiny little startup. If they can land a city in Florida, what the hell is taking you so long to land an island smaller than my neighborhood?"

"Things move slower on this coast, Dad. You know that. It's essentially a small town and—"

"Excuses. I don't want to hear excuses. I want to see results. Two days. That's what you have. If I don't have an answer in two days, I'll fly down there myself and work the entire Gulf Coast. You're a smart girl, Lauren, and my daughter, which means you have everything you need to be a star in this business. If you choose to be. Don't let me down."

Again was the unspoken word. She knew her father's company had been struggling, competing against ever tightening marketing budgets. In recent years, he'd seemed more tired, no longer the barracuda others had accused him of being. Losing Greyhound after he'd been diagnosed with cancer had taken its toll, and all Lauren wanted to do was make it up to him.

"I have a meeting today that should make a big difference," she said. "I'm sorry—"

"Need I remind you that your mistake cost us three million dollars in lost revenue? That's million with an M. I never should have agreed to it in the first place, and you never should have gone off on a vacation without making sure all the Ts were crossed. What were you thinking?"

It was a conversation they'd had a hundred times. No matter how hard she tried to explain, her father didn't want to hear the excuses. He was a man who expected results, not mistakes. "It won't happen again, Dad."

A moment passed with only silence between them. "This company is us," her father said quietly. "You and me. Ever since your mother died, all I've had is McNally and Webster. And you."

Gerald Webster rarely got emotional. Almost never expressed remorse or regret. To hear the note of vulnerability in her father's voice only made Lauren more committed to succeeding. Even though she had been an addendum, not the first thing in his list of what he had. Her father never had been the best at relationships with other people. Even though she knew this, the words hurt all the same. "I know, Dad. You can count on me. I love—"

But her father had already hung up. Lauren swallowed back her disappointment, tucking her phone away just as Carter pulled up in front of the coffee shop.

Great. She didn't even have a second to center herself. The panicky need to prove to her father that she could be the one he relied on, that he didn't need to tax his waning energy by worrying, rose in her throat. She wanted to run at the same time she wanted to stay. Didn't help that Carter hadn't gotten the *not sexy* memo for today.

He was driving a faded green Jeep Wrangler with the roof and doors removed, and his hair had that wind-tossed look she loved. That would have been bad enough to distract her, but then she noticed Carter had on a blue short-sleeved cotton shirt over a pair of striped swim trunks. He'd left the shirt unbuttoned, revealing a magazine-cover-worthy chest.

Holy. Hell.

Carter Malone hadn't just gotten taller and broader in the last decade. He'd become muscular and tan and so damned sexy she almost couldn't breathe when she looked at him. Lauren pushed her hat down more on her head, shading her eyes from his view, then climbed into the Jeep.

"I brought sunscreen," he said. "So if you want to change into something short-sleeved—"

"I'm fine. I'm totally comfortable." A lie. The Florida sun had baked the air into the low nineties already, and a thin bead of sweat ran down the center of Lauren's back. "Let's get going."

He grinned. "Anxious to get our date started?"

"This isn't a date. It's an…agreement between two former friends."

He winced. "Ouch. That sounds about as much fun as a tonsillectomy."

Good. Maybe the more distance she put between the two

of them and the concept of a date, the less she'd be affected by his bare chest. Then Lauren flicked a glance at the tan muscles under the open panels of his shirt, and knew that was a big fat lie.

Carter put the Jeep in gear, then headed down the street. They turned onto 2nd, passing Jenna's shop and leaving the bustle of downtown behind them.

"Where are we going?" she asked.

"It's a surprise." He focused on the road, his eyes hidden behind dark sunglasses. But a smile played on his lips.

Damn the man knew her well.

Despite everything, a little flutter of excitement quickened inside Lauren. She loved surprises, and couldn't remember the last time anyone had planned one for her. Her father had always been staid and practical, her coworkers stressed and serious, and her short marriage strained and distant.

In fact, she didn't think she'd had a surprise since—

Carter showed up outside her window at the Paradise Key resort one hot June evening with a blanket and a six-pack of beer. *It's your birthday*, he'd said. *And I wanted to be the first one to wish you happy birthday and to help you celebrate.*

She'd glanced at the bedside clock. It had been, indeed, her birthday at that exact moment. He'd remembered a short conversation they'd had where she told him she was born on a Saturday night in June, interrupting an awards banquet her parents were attending. As if she'd timed her arrival specifically to prevent her father from accepting his Advertising Executive of the Year award.

That night, she'd snuck out the window with Carter to lay with him under the stars on the beach. They'd kissed, they'd drank, and they'd danced to the music on an old portable radio he'd brought. Hands down, he made that birthday one of the best she could remember.

"It's been a long time since you surprised me," she said, the edges gone from her words. The memory had softened everything inside her, like pouring hot water over butter.

He looked over at her, holding her gaze for a long moment. "I know."

Lauren shifted in her seat, breaking the eye contact before she got all sentimental and romantic. This wasn't a date. It wasn't a trip down Memory Lane. It was a means to an end, nothing more.

Since it was a weekday, traffic was light and they reached the shore in a few minutes. Carter parked, then swung out of the Jeep. He grabbed a blanket and cooler out of the back.

"Picnic?"

"Yup." He handed her the blanket to carry. "Actually, a picnic-plus."

"What's the plus?" Carter just raised an eyebrow at her question. She laughed, then followed him down the sandy path. "Okay, okay. I get it, it's a surprise."

He'd chosen a part of Paradise Key beach rarely visited

by tourists. All the businesses and washed-up shells were closer to the stretch of sand by the resort. This curve of beach, tucked away behind an inlet, was familiar. And private.

"We haven't been here in a long time," Lauren said. When they'd been dating, it had been their favorite spot. He'd taken her here on her birthday all those years ago, brought her here the first time they'd made love, then sat beside her on this very beach and broken her heart at the end of the summer.

"I know," Carter said.

A part of her wondered how many other girls he'd taken here. Had he planned a surprise picnic with someone else? Made love to another woman behind that dune with only the moon for light? Told another woman he loved her, then left her crying and alone? Lauren almost turned around, then saw two paddleboards standing tall and proud in the sand. She stopped. "Paddleboards?"

"Yup." Carter set the blue rectangular cooler down beside one of them. "That's what I said we were doing."

"I thought you were kidding," she said. "Paddleboarding is my favorite thing to do."

"I know." He took the blanket from her, and laid it on top of the cooler. When he straightened, he was somehow closer to her. Much closer. "I remember, Lauren."

Her heart stuttered. Did she want him to kiss her? To leave? To throw her onto that blanket and make love to her until the sun set? Damn it. Why did she keep remembering all the things that were the exact opposite of why she was here? "You remember a lot of things."

"Don't you?"

Staring into his eyes, she could have been seventeen again, running off to the beach with him instead of doing her AP Lit summer reading. Or filling out yet another Ivy league college application. Or practicing violin, decorum, German…whatever her father had decided would serve her well in the future he'd chosen. She'd run off with Carter, suffering more lectures and punishment that summer than any other time in her life because Carter represented everything she wanted but never had. He was flip-flops and sand, beer and irresponsibility.

And sex. No, not sex—*contact*. She'd been drawn to the kryptonite of a simple touch from him. For a girl who had grown up in a cold, results-driven home, the need for physical contact had been almost visceral.

Standing before him now, with the summer sun cooking her in the silly outfit she'd thought could push him away, all Lauren wanted was Carter's touch. The light caress of his hand along her cheek. The slide of his body along the length of hers. Even something as simple and ordinary as Carter taking her hand had been a memory to treasure.

Touch me, she thought. *Reach out and touch me.*

"You ready?" he said.

"Yes." She closed her eyes, wanting, waiting, and—

"Uh, kinda hard to paddleboard with your eyes closed, Lauren."

Damn. Her face heated, and she averted her gaze as she stepped away, pretending the blue and white striped paddleboards were the most interesting things she'd ever seen. "I was just, uh, soaking up the sun." She reached out for the paddleboard, nearly toppling it and falling face-first into the sand. "I haven't been on one of these in a long time."

"Me either."

"You mean you don't bring all your dates here and whisk them off for private 'paddleboarding lessons'?" She made air quotes around the last part, trying to act like she didn't care about the answer.

He stripped off his shirt. She forgot to breathe. "You gonna wear that on the water?"

It took her a second to realize he was talking about her nun attire. Her choice of clothing had been in the event of another kiss, not a day on the water. The masochistic part of her, though, had worn a bikini underneath the long shirt and pants. Because, yeah, maybe she had been hoping for a chance to get nearly naked with Carter.

"No, of course not." She slipped off the shirt, then pulled the drawstring on the pants. They dropped to the sand.

And Lauren noticed Carter had stopped breathing. Ha. That was what he got for not answering her question. She wrapped an arm around one of the paddleboards, then hefted it out of the sand. "You just gonna stand there and stare or are we going to do this?"

He blinked and swallowed. Busted. "Uh, yeah. Sorry."

Well, well. The cool and collected Carter Malone was just as swayed by her charms as she was by his. Perhaps Lauren could use that to her advantage somehow. Play with fire, without actually touching the stove. She grabbed her paddleboard and the oar, then headed down to the water with Carter bringing up the rear.

Lauren waded in a few inches, laid the heavy paddleboard on the smooth ocean, then put the oar down the center. Just as she was getting ready to climb on board, Carter leaned over and whispered in her ear.

"I've never brought any woman here but you, Lauren."

She turned and met his gaze. Neither said a word for a long moment while the water lapped around their knees and the noses of their paddleboards bumped. "Neither have I, Carter," she said, then climbed on board and pushed off, putting as much water between herself and Carter as possible.

Chapter Five

CARTER BARELY NOTICED the bright sun, the sparkly water, or the dolphins cavorting in the distance. The second Lauren had shed her shirt and pants, revealing a tiny bright pink bikini, he'd lost the ability to form a rational thought. Zach, who had dropped off the boards earlier as a favor, would bust a gut laughing at Carter's obvious inattention to the scenery. Honestly, it was a wonder Carter had gotten up on the damned paddleboard without drowning, considering he couldn't tear his eyes away from Lauren's curves.

Not to mention the miles of skin bared by the bikini. The curve of her spine, the flat expanse of her belly, the swell of her breasts. He wanted to touch every damned inch.

But this wasn't a date. They weren't getting involved again. She'd made that abundantly clear. And he would have believed her, too, if he hadn't caught her ogling him.

It was almost laughable how the two of them were trying so hard to keep their distance, to pretend they weren't interested, that nothing existed between them. In the end, though, he needed to remember she was going back to New York and he was staying here, in the town she saw solely as a revenue source. Still, a part of him understood her need to land the account, to do whatever she could to help her father. He had done that himself with the general store. So how could he fault Lauren for the same commitment to her sole remaining parent?

They paddled along for a bit without talking. The silence drove him crazy. It left altogether too much room in his head to picture scenarios with him, Lauren, and the bikini. As well as without the bikini. Definitely more scenarios in his head without than with.

"So...uh, what did you mean by what you said earlier?" he asked her. Yeah, talk about something else. Keep his attention on her face. Not her...well, the rest of her.

"Mean by what?"

"I told you I haven't brought another woman here, and you said neither have I."

"I didn't mean another woman, though I think it sounded that way." Lauren laughed as she gave her oar a push, then switched sides. The board skimmed across the calm water. "I meant I haven't taken anyone else here, man or woman. In fact, I haven't even been back to Paradise Key since that...that summer."

That summer—the one in which they fell in love and made plans for the future, then he'd yanked the rug out from under her and ended their relationship as August began to edge toward September. Yeah, that summer.

At the time, it had seemed like a good idea. He wanted

his future unencumbered. No expectations from his father, no ties to the store, the town, or a relationship. He'd been young and headstrong, determined to carve a path far from here. He'd thought love was easy to find, even easier to keep.

In the end, life had circled him right back to that summer. Karma, or a sadistic side to fate?

"You said you were engaged," Lauren said. leaving a great big unspoken *and* at the end of her sentence.

"I was. Marie was a great person, worked in the same firm I did. At the time I proposed, we wanted the same things out of life. Careers, a condo in the city, a couple of Mercedes in the garage. Then my father got sick, I came down here, and the relationship fell apart." His gaze went to the horizon, to the place where the world seemed to drop off. "Turned out we didn't want the same things out of life."

"It makes sense on paper, though, doesn't it?" Lauren sighed, and paddled for a little bit before she spoke again. "That's why I got married. My father introduced us, and it just seemed like a logical decision."

Carter laughed. "I think all the romance novels say love and marriage are supposed to be the opposite of logical."

Like their summer had been. Every minute of those hot months, his mind had been in a frenzy when it came to Lauren. He'd wanted her by his side, in his arms, beneath his body, almost like an addiction to heroin. Saying goodbye to her had been smart, he'd told himself, but deep down, it'd been as painful as ripping out his own kidney.

"Carter, look. It's a baby!" Lauren's voice was filled with hushed excitement. She pointed to a trio of dolphin dorsal fins a hundred yards away, one noticeably smaller than the other two. "That's incredible."

Change of subject. Good. Perfect timing for getting his mind out of the past and into the present.

"Every time, I'm amazed when I see them," Carter said. He pushed at the water with his oar, bringing the paddleboard closer to the pod. The dolphins circled a small area, undoubtedly feeding on some slower small fish. "If we're very still, they might come up to us."

"Really?"

He nodded. "Just sit down on your board and be very, very quiet." He set down his oar, then lowered his body onto the long flat surface. Lauren did the same beside him. Her paddleboard drifted in his direction, and he caught it, keeping her at his side with a hand on her board.

His hand was inches away from her bare thigh. Her gaze stayed riveted on the dolphins, unaware that a simple shift of her body would give him access to the smooth expanse of her skin. Part of him prayed she shifted. Part of him prayed she didn't.

The pod moved closer as their prey tried to get away. Beside him, Lauren held her breath. So did he.

"Incredible," she whispered.

"Yes, it is." Lauren had a classic beauty, all fine lines and graceful curves. Her hair slid along her neck, long and golden, trailing down with the strings of her bikini top, the pink mingling with the blond, as if begging him to find the ends and tug them free.

"I never see things like this where I live."

"Me either." God, she was beautiful. What had he been thinking, breaking up with her? Surely they could have found a way to stay together. She had grown into a woman who loved fiercely, who had tremendous loyalty, and incredible depth. He had missed all those years with her. Suddenly, he wanted them back.

"I can't stop staring."

"Same here."

"Aren't they just—" Lauren turned to him and stopped talking. "You're not looking at the dolphins at all."

"Nope."

She held his gaze for a breath, maybe two. "Why?"

"Because I've never known another woman like you. Right now, I'm thinking I was the biggest idiot on the planet to let you get away." And a huge idiot for bringing spray sunscreen instead of the cream, which would have given him an excuse to touch her. To be near her, to spend today and tomorrow and the next day right here beside Lauren.

"Carter, I..." The words trailed off, caught in a sigh. "What are we doing here?"

"Exploring...just exploring." He leaned across his board. She hesitated, then shifted toward him. He caught the sweet scent of her perfume, saw the war of desire and caution in her eyes, and stopped caring about all those justifications and reasons that had ran through his head a moment ago. All he saw, all he knew, and all he wanted was Lauren. Just as he was about to kiss her, their boards bumped, Lauren lost her balance, and the two of them tumbled into the water.

The dolphins bolted, leaving Carter with heavy regret and a sense he'd just screwed up something rare.

BY THE TIME they brought the paddleboards back to the beach, both Lauren and Carter were thirsty and starving. She pretended to feel a sunburn starting, and slipped her shirt over her bikini. For a moment there on the water, with the two of them barely clothed and nothing separating them but a few inches of board, a rush of desire overthrew Lauren's common sense. Carter had come closer, she'd neared him, and in that space, the heat had multiplied until she stopped thinking rationally.

If they hadn't fallen in the water, she had no doubt the kiss between them would have been legendary. Carter knew her, knew her mouth, knew her body, knew how to tease and tempt her. And the way he had been looking at her...

She sat on the blanket, tucked her knees under the over-sized shirt, and drew them to her knees. Thinking about that did no good. It only led down the very path she was trying to avoid. The one where Carter kissed her again, and the two of them—very, very alone in this private little section of beach—found out if the present was anywhere near as amazing as the past had been.

Well, most of the past. The way things had ended that summer…that wasn't something Lauren wanted to repeat. So she wasn't going to kiss him. Not today. Not again. Not at all.

"I'm starved. I brought some lunch. Hope you like it."

"I like that you planned ahead." She smirked. Lauren normally excelled at getting her job done, but when it came to the details of regular life, she dropped the ball more than she caught it. Hence the dead plants in her apartment and the empty fridge she had at home. "If you relied on me, we would have gone hungry."

"I remember." He chuckled. "When the zombie apocalypse comes, I know not to count on you to stock the shelter. Remember that time you planned a picnic for us?"

"And I brought two water bottles, a package of cookies, and a single napkin? I swear I put sandwiches in there." She laughed. "I was so distracted that day."

Distracted by him. By the crazy rush to be together that had consumed her every thought that summer. Had he felt the same thing? Did he feel that way now?

"Good thing I've got us covered today." Carter opened the cooler, handed her a water bottle, then began to lay out sandwiches, chips, and paper plates. A boat cut through the water in the distance.

"Thank you. I'm glad you thought of the food, the paddleboards, everything."

"I figured you'd want at least some time to be on vacation, even if it's only for today."

Damn Carter for being so thoughtful. That summer, he'd been the same—always making sure he had an extra sweatshirt in his car for chilly nights, being sure to ask her if she was hungry or thirsty—that was Carter. Sweet. Considerate. Tempting.

All she wanted to do was lie back on the plaid flannel blanket and turn her face to the sun with the warmth of Carter beside her. To recapture the magic of that summer, the sense of freedom and fun.

Then she thought of her father's call. Two days. It was all she had to come up with a miracle. She couldn't waste one of them living in the past. Not when her father was depending on her to make it right.

Lauren unwrapped her sandwich, and took a bite. A sweet and savory combination of turkey and cranberry jam on crispy rye met her tongue. "This is awesome."

"I can't take the credit. I picked them up at Deli 2983. Miriam is the owner there, a rough and tumble New Jersey transplant, but an amazing chef. She has the most inventive sandwiches I've ever seen."

She took a long sip of water, waving off Carter's offer of a beer. All she needed was a little alcohol to tip the desire running through her body from the *Not Gonna Happen* column into *Let's Do This*. Carter shrugged, popped the top of his beer, and took a deep drink.

"So…" Lauren said, forcing her mind away from Carter's bare chest and back to her job. "I wanted to talk to you about the marketing idea I had. If you listen to my ideas, maybe you can see the benefit and—"

"Why are you doing this?"

"What do you mean? This is my job, Carter. We talked about this." Granted, a job she had barely focused on since she ran into Carter again, but that was changing. Right now. For sure.

"Exactly. Why are you doing this job?" He propped himself on one elbow, stretching his length down his side of the blanket. Carter settled into the easy pace of life in Paradise Key as easy as fitting the last piece into a jigsaw puzzle, and a part of her wanted to curve her body against his and feel the same ease. "I thought you hated marketing, and wanted to rebel and go to art school."

"That was a foolish dream." Once upon a time, Lauren had spent every spare moment sketching. Trees, birds, buildings, people, anything she could capture with pencils and pastels. Then her father had found her stack of drawings, and spent an hour berating her for wasting so many precious hours. From there on out, the pressure from him to excel in school, to make smart use of every minute of her life, had multiplied. He'd been overprotective and demanding, as if he'd poured all his energy into the one family member he had left.

Sometimes she thought the hole her mother's death had left in her father's life was too wide and deep to ever fill again, not with his work or with an infinite number of achievements from his daughter. From the day she came home from the funeral, she had felt a constant need to watch over her father, to step into her mother's role, to make sure he was happy and protect him from another heartache like that. Until she'd arrived in Paradise Key and told herself it was her time to spread her wings. When she'd gone to her father and said she was leaving home to go live with Carter—

He'd broken down. It was only the second time she'd ever seen her father cry. She didn't want there to be a third time.

But that was too much to encapsulate in a single sentence. So she defaulted to the excuse she had used for three decades. "Going to art school wasn't practical," she said. "I would have never made a living as an artist. Working for my father lets me combine art with my job, so it's a nice substitute."

Except she hated her job. She had never found the same joy in it that her father did.

"Seems to me," Carter said before taking a sip of beer, "that the overachiever in you is still there."

"And what's wrong with that? Overachievers get things done. Overachievers become successes." She could have been reciting a speech from her father, only Lauren had been anything but an overachiever at McNally and Webster. Yes, she had worked hard, put in nights and weekends, foregone vacations, but her lack of passion meant her work never reached the same level of accolades as others' work did. "Overachievers—"

"Are rarely truly happy." Carter leaned closer, and his gaze locked on hers. "Are you truly happy, Lauren? In your high-powered career in the busiest city on earth? Working for your father? Who drove you crazy and made your life miserable, if I remember right."

"Of course I'm happy. Why wouldn't I be?" She drank deep from her water bottle, but it wasn't enough to fill the empty space in her gut. Not because Carter had a point. Not because she wondered the same thing about her father, and about her own future. Because she was hungry, that was all.

"Really? Because I know you, Lauren, and you don't look happy or content."

"You know who I used to be, Carter. I've changed since then."

He tipped his beer in her direction. "Ah, you have a point. We've both changed since that summer."

They had. She'd given up on the childish idea of running away. Instead, she'd gone to work for her father, taking the job he had groomed her for all her life. He'd invested so much in her, and in preparing her to take over someday. When she'd run off that weekend a few months ago, and the Greyhound campaign had fallen apart, she'd let him down once again. Okay, so maybe she didn't really love her job the way her father did, and maybe a part of her dreaded Monday mornings and rebelled inside against the meetings and deadlines. But that didn't mean she was going to invest in silly things like an art career or a man who had no staying power. She was no longer a foolish teenage girl who thought a summer romance could become something permanent. And Carter had become...

Well, hot as hell. And settled. Sweet, too. Ironically, they were once again from two different worlds, and there wasn't any sense in trying to combine them. Once upon a time, she'd thought she wanted what Carter had here in Paradise Key. She remembered being so envious of him, and so frustrated he couldn't see the freedom and peace he had in this town.

And now things had come full circle. Lauren had the office in the high-rise, far from the island she'd once thought would be her forever home, and Carter had come back to the very place he'd wanted to leave.

She cleared her throat. Work, she had to think about work and nothing else, especially not the what-ifs from today.

As much as Carter saw her as the enemy when it came to Paradise Key, she did love this little town. She'd done a lot of thinking about what would work best to serve her purposes, yet also preserve what Carter and Eloise so ardently protected. "You know, I'm not the enemy here when it comes to helping Paradise Key boost its tourism presence."

He scoffed. "I don't know about that. Every marketing firm that has ever come into this town and tried to sell us, has wanted to promote it as something it isn't. There's more money in being a party town, they say, or add some gambling and you'll attract a wealthier crowd. Paradise Key doesn't want or need any of that. I'm not saying we couldn't use a little more business. Just that we don't want to gain it at the cost of what makes us special."

The ocean curled into the cove that held just the two of them. The setting rejuvenated her, wiped away all the worries she'd had on the flight down here, and early this morning. If a visit to Paradise Key could do that for Lauren, it could do it for anyone. "What if we marketed Paradise Key as a place to wind down, to get away from the stress of worrying about retirement accounts, income taxes, and all the big stuff? Then it might be a slightly different take on the way other companies market Florida. Fill your mind with images of this," she waved toward the ocean, "and it's as good as meditating for an entire day. I thought I could use an image of someone doing yoga, but her mind is on her 401k plan contributions. Then she comes here, and her mind is only on relaxing."

Carter thought about her words for a second, then he nodded. "That's actually a great idea. But how do you know it will work?"

"We'd get a focus group and—"

"No, I mean, how do you know it will work if you don't try it yourself?"

She arched a brow. "What have we been doing all day?"

"Mostly? We've been arguing about why you should do all the marketing for Paradise Key."

"We have not. We've been—" Almost kissing. Thinking about sex. More of the latter than anything else. "Paddle-boarding."

"Yeah, that too. But mostly, we've been talking and debating." He grinned. "So let's stop talking and start doing." He got to his feet, then put out his hand. "Come on, Lauren."

"Where?"

"To the place where you stop worrying about your job and your 401k plan." He wagged his hand in her direction.

She debated staying where she was. Continuing to work on him, plead her case, show him the wisdom of working with McNally and Wester. She had no doubt if she could keep Carter's attention, she could convince him and get him on her side. If not, she was going to have to circumvent Carter and try to go to Eloise and Merle herself again.

Two days, that was all she had. And she was spending one of them here. With Carter. Was that choice going to ruin everything?

"We agreed this wasn't a date. That we could talk about—"

"And we did. I think you have a great idea, but I also

think this town might not be ready even for something as simple as that. Paradise Key is more like a family neighborhood than a town, Lauren. You have to understand that."

"Carter, I do. I've been here, remember? I love this town, too. It has some of my best memories. Trust me—I don't want to do anything that will harm Paradise Key. No gimmicks, no contests, no silly marketing ideas. Just one that captures the best of this place and brings in enough business to help improve the town's bottom line. For you, for your dad, for everyone."

He thought about that for a moment, his gaze on hers. "You really mean that?"

"Of course I do. Trust me." Did she mean about more than just the marketing campaign? She didn't know, didn't want to answer that. "I'm not doing this for money. Or to change this town. I'm doing it for my father. To ease his mind some, to prove to him that I...I can be depended on. It's about family—my family—not ruining Paradise Key. Please believe me about that."

"I trust you, Lauren. I always have." He put up a finger to stop her reply. "But that only works if you trust me in return and agree to have some fun. Come on, Lauren," he said, his voice low and dark, "take a chance. Live a little, no, a lot."

"Carter—"

"The Lauren I remember wouldn't have hesitated. This Lauren is...stuffy."

It bothered her more than she liked to admit that he saw her as stuffy. Yet, Lauren couldn't remember the last time she'd had fun. The last time she hadn't been stressed about her job. She'd worked weekends and vacations for so long it seemed wrong to do anything else. So okay, maybe she wasn't finding as much joy in her days as she used to, but that was part of being a grownup. Right? "I'm not stuffy. I'm still fun."

His smile quirked the right side of his mouth. "Oh yeah? Prove it."

Prove it. Carter had dared her with those same words all those years ago. They'd met at the ice cream parlor when she'd slipped away from her aunt's watchful eye to order a cone. He'd asked her out, she'd told him that her father and aunt would never let her go, and he'd dared her to sneak out after they went to bed. She'd demurred, he'd teasingly called her a chicken, and she'd said she was anything but. Carter had leaned in, whispering in her ear above the din of orders being called and children laughing. *Prove it.*

She remembered climbing out of the window at the resort and dropping to the dewy grass. Her bare feet left deep impressions as she raced across the lawn and down to the beach, her heart in her throat, as if the devil himself were on her heels. All her life, she'd been the good girl, staying in on weekends to study or put extra time into a school project. She went to bed on time, ate her vegetables, and never missed a curfew.

Until she met Carter.

That summer had been amazing. She'd been drawn to Carter because he made her laugh, made her want to take a risk, and most of all, because he was the most fun she'd ever had. Every day they had together had been better than the one before. She'd never dated anyone else quite like Carter. Losing him had left a hole in her life that had never really been filled by another man.

"Remember that summer?" Carter asked. "That was all you wanted, you told me, was to buck all those rules and expectations and just *be*. To jump off the cliff and not look back. Just be with me today, Lauren."

His hand was inches away, along with the temptation to shirk that heavy mantle of expectations and responsibilities. To leave her stress and worries on the beach, just for a moment.

Prove it. The thought of that sounded heavenly. It sounded risky. It sounded like exactly what she needed to do. If there was one thing she'd learned from the death of Lily, it was that life was too damned short to spend it worrying about work. What would it hurt? No one would know. She'd spend an hour, no more.

Lauren glanced at the sparkling blue water, then back at the man she used to love, and decided she surely deserved an hour of living in the past before she got back to the present.

Chapter Six

DAMN, HE LOVED the sound of her laugh.

He'd tugged Lauren down to the water, then into the Gulf. The waves splashed around them, and she let out a shriek because it was cold, then the shriek gave way to laughter, and she started splashing him. He splashed her back, the two of them scooping up more and more water at each other, like they were a couple of kids at the town pool. It was that first summer all over again. For a moment, he felt eighteen, head over heels in love, with the world stretched out before them.

He charged toward her. "I'm going to dunk you!"

She laughed and scrambled back. "Not if I get away first!" Lauren pivoted and ran through the shallow water, giving him one hell of a view of her rear profile.

He caught up to her, grabbed her arm, and spun her against his chest. Her skin met his, and all the pretty resolutions he'd made about keeping her at a distance ended. He could feel her breasts on his chest, the tempting dip of her waist under his hand. God, he had missed her. Missed the sound of her voice, the scent of her perfume, and most of all, the feel of her beneath him.

He pulled her close, then leaned down and kissed her. He didn't bother with pleasantries. He just kissed her, hard and fast and hot.

Like a switch had been flipped, Lauren responded in kind, her arms snaking around his back, her body pressing against his. When his tongue slid into her mouth, she answered with her own, dancing with his mouth. She let out a little mew, and he stopped caring they weren't getting involved again and she was all wrong for him. He didn't think about tomorrow or next week or next month; all he wanted, all he knew, was right now. He lowered them, until she was beneath him at the edge of the water, the incoming tide washing onto them, then back again. She was warm and soft and everything he had missed over the last ten years.

"Damn it, Lauren. I still can't resist you."

"Then don't." She surged up toward him, wrapping her arms around his neck. Her eyes danced with merriment and desire. "Just for a little while, Carter, let's just…forget."

Forget they were broken up. Forget she wanted him to help her turn this sleepy little town into a tourist mecca. Forget that even after all this time, they still lived on opposite sides of life.

He knew it was crazy. Rational thought said to step away. But when it came to Lauren, rational thought had never prevailed. Despite everything, she was the one woman he'd never been able to resist. And never forgotten.

"I never did, Lauren," he whispered. He slid a hand under the bikini top to cup the round softness of her breast. She gasped and arched beneath him. Carter tore his mouth away from hers and trailed kisses along her neck, down the sweet scoop of her chest, until he reached her breast. He sucked the tip into his mouth, knowing exactly how much pressure Lauren liked and how she would respond.

Beneath him, she moaned and clawed at his back. He switched his mouth to the other side, then kissed a path to her belly button, to the arch of her hips. He was hard and she was soft, and they were very, very much alone. He reached for the strings that held the bottom of her bikini in place.

Lauren gasped. "Carter, oh, God, Carter, I want...Oh yes, please do..." Her hands were in his hair, her body meeting his.

He wanted to tear that tiny, sexy bikini off her and make love to her right here on the sand. To taste her, fill her with himself, and ease the ache that had begun the minute she walked back into his life.

But if he did that, he wanted it to be because Lauren wanted him in her life as much as he wanted her in his. For something other than her job. For...well, forever.

"I can't." He readjusted her bikini top, then sat back, half in the water, half out. The cool water eased his discomfort. A little. Maybe he was crazy, because he was sitting here with a very willing woman wanting more than just a one-night stand.

She blinked at him, then sat up on her elbows. "What do you mean, you can't? You sure seemed like you wanted to a second ago."

"I did. I do." He shook his head and cursed. "I want you to know this isn't what I came here for. It's not what I intended when I packed the lunch and ordered the paddleboards."

"Then what did you want, Carter?"

"What I foolishly let go all those years ago." His gaze met hers, and he knew if she said the word, he would be right back on top of her. It took every ounce of his willpower to keep the distance between them. When he was eighteen, maybe one night would have been enough. But he was an adult now, an adult who had seen what was possible between two people, and who wanted that for himself. "You and me, not for a summer, Lauren. For a lot longer than that."

She didn't say anything for a long moment. Then she got to her feet, brushing sand off her legs as she did. "If I remember right, you had that once…and you let it go. Only a fool walks back into a mistake. And I'm not a fool, Carter. Not anymore."

She strode back to the flannel blanket, pulled on her clothes and hat, and began packing up the picnic. He followed along, telling himself this was the best choice all around. They only exchanged a few words as they loaded up his Jeep, then left the water and the sand and Lauren's laughter behind.

ELOISE WAS NO easier to budge today than she had been a few days ago. After Carter dropped her off, Lauren had showered off the sand, rubbed moisturizer on her slight sunburn, then gotten dressed in another Anne Klein suit and pumps. For the first time since she'd started her job at McNally and Webster with a wardrobe carefully culled from the racks at Nordstrom, Lauren felt like her clothes didn't fit. The silky cornflower blue blouse and dark-gray hound's-tooth pattern skirt chafed at her skin. The heels made her toes ache. And tucking her hair into its usual chignon felt foreign.

It was too much sun. That was all. Not her mind returning over and over again to that wild moment with the sand and surf and Carter. And how close she had come to falling for him all over again.

That would have been a massive mistake. He might have been fun that one summer, and had her considering ditching her perfect, structured life full of expectations, but in the end, he'd broken her heart and proven a life of daring led nowhere good. Today, she'd been foolish enough to let a moment of weakness sweep her up into all that again.

Never again. If she did that, she would be letting her father down. He was counting on her. She was going to concentrate entirely on why she was still here in town, and no matter what it took, find a way to land this account, without having to go through Carter Malone.

"So, Mrs. Josephs," Lauren said after making her case to Eloise, "what do you think of hiring McNally and Webster to be your marketing partners?"

"I'm so sorry, Miss Webster, but I talked your idea over with Merle, and he agrees with me." Eloise gestured toward Merle, who looked like he hadn't moved from his desk in the last week. He had his feet propped up, head tipped back, snores coming regular and loud. "We both think Paradise Key doesn't need some fancy marketing campaign to bring in tourists."

Lauren smiled. Again. "Every town that relies on tourism could use a marketing campaign. We could start small, maybe highlight the shops downtown, because I noticed business is a little slow for those shops and I'm sure they need the sales to—"

Eloise thrust a round tin in Lauren's direction. "Blondie?"

It took a second for Lauren to realize the one-woman Paradise Key Welcome Wagon was offering her yet another dessert. She started to refuse, then remembered Carter's advice about Eloise's baked goods. "Why yes, thank you."

Eloise gestured to the chair across from her desk. After Lauren sat, Eloise set the tin inside its lid and placed the container between them, as if this were afternoon tea between friends. "Carter tells me you used to spend your summers here."

Apparently having a tie to Paradise Key could give Lauren a bit of an edge. If that was the case, she'd recite every memory she had from those summers with the girls. "I did. Which is why I would be a great choice to help market the—"

"Tut, tut." Eloise put up a finger. "I think quite the opposite, Miss Webster. Because you have spent time here, you know how incredible Paradise Key is. And what makes it incredible is that it's a small town. With small-town folks and small-town values. If we start tooting our horn to the rest of the world, before you know it, we won't be a small town anymore. We'll be a…God forbid, Miami." She shuddered.

All of her career, Lauren had helped small businesses grow into large companies that dominated their industry. Every business owner she and the team at McNally and Webster met with had wanted more—more exposure, more customers, more sales. Not even one had said *let's stay small*. To Lauren, Eloise was speaking a foreign language.

Carter wasn't kidding when he'd said the town wasn't going to welcome McNally and Webster with open arms. Right now, that meant Lauren had two choices—go back to Carter or convince Eloise, without the input of Carter. Considering her body was still simmering with desire whenever she thought about Carter, Lauren decided to go back to him would be a bad choice. At least not until after she'd had a cold shower. Or ten.

Besides, Carter wanted something out of her she couldn't

give. There was no way she was going to commit to this town, to him, to anything. Not until she was sure her father and his company were going to be okay.

"Thank you so much for the wonderful brownie," Lauren said. "But—"

"Blondie. It's a blondie. Like you." Eloise smiled. "Not a smidge of chocolate in it. You should try it."

Lauren took a bite, if only to keep playing the *I'm just a local like you* angle. A butterscotch flavor smoothed across her tongue. Wow. Carter was right. Eloise could really bake. "It's delicious."

"Thank you. They're Merle's favorite bar cookies. He just raves about them every time I bring them into the office."

Lauren cast a dubious look at Merle. He snarfled, coughed, then went back to snoring. "Perhaps I could talk to Mr. Higgins when he is back from vacation, along with you two, and explain—"

"Miss Webster." Eloise's friendly face pinched and narrowed. "I appreciate your obstinate efforts to get Paradise Key to work with some kind of fancy big city marketing campaign but…" She took in a breath, let it out. "We are not interested."

"Not even a smidge?" Lauren kept a bright smile on her face. The friendly, *work with me, we're on the same team* smile that had worked a hundred other times.

"Not even a smidge of a smidge." She yanked the tin

back, snapped the lid on top, and tucked the container under the desk. "Now, if our meeting is concluded, Merle and I have some work to do today."

Lauren suspected Merle hadn't done a thing since 1972. As for Gary Higgins, the third member of the tourism board, the sign on his closed office door still said ON VACATION. That left Eloise, who definitely wasn't going to budge.

Lauren got to her feet, thanked Eloise for the blondies, and kept that teamwork smile on her face until after the door shut behind her. Two days to pull this off before her father probably came down here and did the job himself because he was tired of her not performing at work. Like he had everything else in her life, he would undoubtedly micromanage this, too. Day one was a complete bust. Damn.

The sun was bright, the temp lingering in the high eighties. It was, as Carter had promised, a perfect day for the beach. Only a few hours ago, she'd been there, with him, ditching her responsibilities just like she'd ditched her father and his rules that summer. She'd endured dozens of lectures and a half-serious threat to send her to an all-girls' boarding school, but at the time, she'd thought it had been worth it to be with Carter. To live another life than the one she'd always known.

Until he broke her heart, and she'd done the only thing she could to ease the pain—she'd worked, burying her head in books and reports and college applications. In time, the memories of that summer faded, and the temptation to run from her life disappeared.

Except on days like today, when she could catch the scent of the ocean in the air, feel the leftover grains of sand between her toes, and hear the excited calls of seagulls. Lauren wanted to forget about her job, run barefoot across the lawn of the resort, and straight into Carter's arms.

Insanity. She needed to do that like she needed to grow an extra nose.

Lauren pulled out her phone, then scrolled through her emails and text messages. Sofia asked her to get drinks tonight, Jenna wondered how she was doing, and Eve was begging for the scoop on Carter. Lauren said yes to the drinks, she was doing fine, and there was no scoop. The words bordered on the truth—if that border was as wide as the Grand Canyon.

She turned the corner, passing JavaStop, the quirky coffee shop in downtown Paradise Key she'd been in earlier, just as Tyson Braddock, the town commissioner she'd been trying to get a meeting with, emerged from the building. Lauren tucked her phone in her purse and put on her *we're a team* smile.

"Six o'clock, Lorelei," Tyson called over his shoulder to the woman behind the counter of the coffee shop. "I'll be on time. I assume you will be, too?"

"Of course, honey. See you tonight!" She gave him a little wave and a smile, but Tyson had already shut the door. Lauren had heard the coffee shop owner was dating the town commissioner. Didn't exactly seem like a match made in heaven, especially given Tyson's critical tone, but Lauren was the last to judge someone else's relationship, considering she'd ruined her short-lived marriage and had rebuffed Carter, a man who actually wanted a relationship, a few hours earlier.

"Mr. Braddock," Lauren said. "So nice to run into you."

Tyson's brows knitted. Tyson was one of those pretty men, wearing a neat, pale gray skinny-legged suit, a pink tie, and shoes so shiny, Lauren could see her reflection. His hair was short and neat, held in place with some kind of gel, and he had the pampered look of a man who didn't know how to change his own oil. "Do I know you?"

"I'm sorry, no, you don't." She thrust out her hand. "Lauren Webster. I'm here in town for a few days. I came down after my friend Lily died, for the funeral."

"Ah yes, I remember hearing about that. Car accident, right? Such a tragedy." He shook his head.

"Yes, it was. And so sudden." Lauren drew in a breath. Even mentioning Lily made her heart ache. It still didn't seem real, and Lauren knew there would always be a missing piece in their group of friends. She shook off the thoughts, trying to refocus on the opportunity before her. "Anyway, you're just the man I wanted to talk to. While I was in town, I thought I'd run a few ideas by the tourism board for increasing the vacation revenue in Paradise Key. But I'm not really getting anywhere. I was hoping with your input, perhaps the tourism board would be more open to working with a marketing agency."

Tyson leaned against a street pole and crossed his arms over his chest. "I'm always in favor of expansion and bringing in more money to this town. Even if not everyone else sees the wisdom of that."

"Exactly!" Finally, someone in Paradise Key who didn't associate the word *marketing* with *spawn of the devil.* "I work for McNally and Webster. They're a firm out of New York City, and most of our work has been with major corporate clients in the northeast. Gillette, Reebok, General Electric. However, two years ago, we started a new division that focused solely on tourism, mainly in the New England area. We see these jobs as a natural extension of our work with leisure brands."

"New England?" Tyson scoffed. "They're not Florida. How will that give you any idea what we need down here?"

"I used to vacation here in Paradise Key. I have a soft spot for this town." She gave him her *work with me* smile.

"I'm listening."

About time someone did. Lauren tamped down her excitement before her desperation showed. "I'd love to sit down with you and share some of my ideas. I really think if Paradise Key worked with the right marketing firm, business could boom here. The resort—"

"Eyesore, if you ask me."

Lauren bristled at the word. Maybe it was a sudden burst

of sentimentality, but the Paradise Key Resort held all her memories with Jenna, Eve, Sofia, Lily, and even Carter. Whenever she remembered those summers, the resort always held that tint of nostalgia, like a sepia photograph in her mind. "I agree the resort could use a buyer who would be willing to do some updates. But you're not going to find that if the town isn't attracting tourists. A smart marketing campaign will bring more visitors and thus, more income to everyone."

"I've been saying that for years. However, this town has a limited budget." He leaned toward her, and his gaze narrowed. "How much for this 'smart' marketing campaign?"

As opposed to the dumb one? Lauren kept that *we're a team* smile plastered on her face. "Well, I don't have any numbers right now. It all depends on what you and the town decide to do. Ads in airports for instance, maybe a radio spot in the northeast during the winter, some television—"

"All three of those scream expensive. I am a hundred percent behind expansion and growth, but not if it comes at a high cost. Your firm is in New York, you say?"

She nodded.

"Everything in that city has a big price tag. I'm thinking of something more…conservative in cost. But not conservative in approach. I want something splashy, bold. Something that screams come to Paradise Key and spend your money." He laughed. "Sort of like what they do for Vegas, you know? Grab people's attention. Make it memorable as hell."

Lauren had thought Tyson Braddock was her ticket to circumventing the tourism board. But he was like so many potential clients—wanting the entire meal on the appetizer budget. "So basically, you'd like a big, splashy marketing campaign at a bargain price?"

"Frankly, yes. I'm on the commission. It's my job to watch the dollars and cents. So if we spent, say, five thousand dollars, what would that give us?"

Her father wouldn't cross the street for five thousand dollars, never mind fly key staff down to Florida to design a campaign. Of course, she'd known going into this that Paradise Key was small potatoes compared to what her father's firm usually took on. But it was a potato Lauren was confident she could handle. One she had an affinity for. If there was ever a place to kick off a new start for her career, this would be it.

Maybe she could get Tyson to agree to a higher dollar amount. A town this size could afford a bigger budget, especially given how much of the residents depended on tourism for their incomes. Right now, though, Braddock wasn't seeing or thinking that. Lauren's heart sank. "That's a really low number, Mr. Braddock. Maybe we could come up with a more realistic budget that can work for the town."

Tyson reached into his pocket, pulled out a business card, and handed it to her. "Call me when you have that realistic number."

He was about to leave. She couldn't let that happen.

Two days, and one was nearly done. She thought again of her father, of his soft words about them being a team. She stepped forward, laid a quick touch on Tyson's arm. "Mr. Braddock, if you could give me just twenty minutes later today, I think I could show you the numbers on how your investment can benefit the entire bottom line of Paradise Key. Town, shops, residents."

He considered her for a moment. "Entire bottom line, you say?"

"Yes."

"You have yourself a meeting. I'll see you in my office at," he flipped out his wrist, "quarter to three. Sound good? But I want to hear something splashy and cool, none of this home and hearth kind of stuff."

"Sure, sure. Thank you." She tucked the card away, said goodbye to Tyson, and watched him continue down the sidewalk. He greeted every person he saw with the kind of fake friendliness of a politician. A proponent of growth, but only if it came cheap and easy.

Lauren had hadn't come this far and worked this hard to lose now. It might take a little more effort to show Tyson how the campaign she'd talked about with Carter could work, as opposed to his idea for splashy and crazy, but she could do it. She wasn't going back to New York until she landed the Paradise Key account, blondies and snicker-doodles be damned.

Chapter Seven

CARTER HEADED INTO Malone's Market a little after two, holding up a hand in his father's direction before the question could be voiced. "Don't ask."

"I thought you were taking the day off to spend with Lauren. What happened?"

"What part of 'don't ask' didn't you hear?" Carter shook his head, letting out a low curse. From the second he'd dropped Lauren off at the resort, he'd been frustrated. He could blame it on the sun exposure, but truth was, he'd expected his plans to go another direction. What direction, he wasn't sure. But definitely not down the *drop me off, we're done today* way. Maybe a part of him had been trying to recapture the past, like some melancholy teenager who needed closure or something stupid like that. "Sorry, Dad. The day didn't turn out like I hoped. Thanks for filling in for me. I can work the rest of the afternoon if you want to go home."

"Don't worry about it. If I go home, your mother is going to want help with the garden. As much as I love her, I'm not a big fan of planting azaleas." Roger Malone came out from behind the counter, ducked down the aisle of freezer cases, reached inside and pulled something out, then held it toward his son. "Dreamsicle?"

"That's not going to work."

"Sure it is." His father tick-tocked the orange and vanilla ice cream back and forth. "Whenever you had a bad day at school or got a bad grade, I'd—"

"Give me a Dreamsicle, then sit with me on the bench out front and we'd talk about it." Carter chuckled. "I'm not twelve anymore."

Roger shrugged. The amiable smile that was part and parcel of Roger's personality curved across his face, making him look younger than his gray hair and sixty-two years announced. His brown eyes sparkled. "Store's dead right now. The sun is shining. And look, what do you know, the bench is free."

Carter knew when to admit defeat. Besides, he was kind of hungry. "Give me that."

His father handed over the ice cream, chuckling as he followed his son outside. They settled beside each other on the wooden bench, both a little older and wider than the last time they'd done this, but still fitting comfortably on the well-worn seat. How many conversations had Carter had with his father in this very spot? It was where he'd learned about the birds and the bees, and where he'd been when he told his father he was heading to Chicago and not coming back. And then, years later, where he sat and prayed while his father clung to life in a hospital bed. For all of Carter's life, the bench had sat there, solid, predictable, and comforting.

"Maybe I'm an idiot for trying to resurrect the past." Carter sighed. "We were teenagers when we dated, and maybe it's true what they say. You can't go back again."

"No, you can't. But you can go forward." Roger leaned forward and propped his arms on his knees. "Did I ever tell you the story about how your mother dumped me?"

Carter chuckled as he unwrapped the Dreamsicle. "Ma dumped you? I thought you two fell madly in love on your first date and got married like two months later."

"Three. But yeah, that's the story we tell everyone. It's just not the whole story."

Carter sat back, eating the ice cream before it melted in the warm sun. He did kind of feel like a kid again, but right now, that was okay. He'd had a hell of a day. "So, why did Ma break up with you?"

"Short answer? I was an idiot." Roger chuckled. "Your mother was and still is the best thing to ever happen to me. But in keeping with being an idiot, I didn't realize it at the time. When I met her, she was working behind the counter at the hardware store that used to be across the street. She was twenty, home for college break, and maybe the most stunning woman in the world. Long black hair, the biggest green eyes I've ever seen." He shook his head. "Even now, I can see her smile, and it makes my heart sing."

Carter laughed. "Dad, you sound almost poetic. You

never sound poetic."

"And I'm not, except when it comes to your mother. I asked her out, and at first, she said no. She had a fella back at college who was sweet on her, and she wanted to see where that could lead, she said. I told her she had three months until she went back there, and what would it hurt to give me a chance? We could call it quits in the fall, and she could go back to the other guy. Short, easy, nothing complicated. That's what I wanted in those days."

"A summer romance, huh?"

"Yep. Just like you and Lauren. In this town, we see plenty of those, and I have to admit, I had a few myself before I got married. Pretty girls come to town, then go back home a few weeks later. Spring break romances, summer romances, flames dying almost as soon as they ignite. But some romances are different. Special."

"Like you and Ma."

Roger nodded. "I didn't realize that early on, though I did know she was pretty incredible. On our first date, I took your mom to dinner and a movie. I was working here, for old Mr. Forlin, who owned the place then."

The original owner of Malone's Market, back when it was known as Paradise Key Five and Dime, had been a wiry, grizzled man with a long beard and a short temper. "I remember him. He gave grumpy a whole new definition."

"Ah, that he did. It's always puzzled me why a man who can't stand people went into a business that caters to the public. Anyway, back then, I wasn't making more than a buck an hour, if that. So I took your mom to a little diner that used to be on Third Street. It's gone now, but back then, it was *the* place to go if you were young and broke. Which we were." Roger smiled, then leaned back against the bench. "She had a turkey club, and a bag of salt and vinegar flavored potato chips. She had on this real pretty pink dress, too. I think they call it a sundress, with the straps instead of sleeves? Anyway, she was beautiful. I felt way out of my league, but I was captivated and determined not to let her get away. After the movie, I walked her home and kissed her, and thought, man, she is amazing. I asked her out on a second date, and a third, before we even got to her door."

Carter chuckled. "She said yes, I presume?"

"Yup. We dated for a couple of weeks. Courted, really, which means no hanky-panky. I thought sure her father would shoot me on the spot if I did anything other than kiss his daughter. Your grandpa was protective as hell, but I can see why. If we'd ever had a daughter half as special as your mother is, I'd have put up a ten-foot security wall around the house to keep young men like I was out of the yard. Your mother made me laugh, oh how she made me laugh. All I could think about was seeing her again. Then Valerie Halstead came to town."

Carter thought back, but the name didn't ring a bell. "She's not a local, right?"

"Nope. She was here on vacation with her folks, like

Lauren and her friends were when you met her. One afternoon in July, Valerie walked into the general store, ordered an ice cream float—we used to make those back then before the Bonners opened their ice cream shop—and told me in no uncertain terms that she was interested in me and wanted a date."

Carter thought of Heidi's overly forward move at the restaurant last night. Any other time, he would have taken the waitress's flirting as an invitation. But with Lauren back, Carter realized he was tired of the fluff and wanted something more. Something memorable. Something rare. Someone who would be there through thick and thin. Once upon a time, that had been Lauren. Now? He wasn't so sure. "And how did you react?"

"Like any idiot at twenty-one. All I saw was a pretty girl who wanted me, and I thought I was too young to be tied to one woman. I didn't want to settle down. I wanted to play the field, sow some oats. I was stupid enough to tell your mother I thought we should see other people. She told me I could see anyone I wanted, but I would no longer be seeing her if I did. We broke up, and I took Valerie out a few times. I kept thinking your mother would be back—in those days, I didn't have the dinner belly or the wrinkles and fancied myself a catch—because we got on so well. But no, she was madder than a cat in a monsoon."

Carter's mother had a temper that rarely made an appearance. He had seen it a few times—when the mechanic overcharged her for a car repair, when Carter's second grade teacher said he lacked discipline, and whenever anyone said a mean word about the people she loved. "I can only imagine Ma's reaction."

"She stopped talking to me entirely. Started going out with Hank McLeary." Roger's lips thinned. "I saw them together a couple times, holding hands and laughing. Damned near killed me. And I damned near killed him for asking her out."

Hank McLeary was a big barrel-chested man with a deep laugh and a fly-tying business that kept him occupied in retirement. He'd been over the house so much when Carter was young that he thought of Hank as a de facto uncle. "But you and Hank are buddies now, right?"

Roger waved a hand. "Yeah. All that stuff is water under the bridge. But back then, I wanted to knock his lights out for taking my girl on the town. I went up to him and told him so, right in front of your mother. Before Hank could say a word, your mother said, 'Don't waste your time, Roger. Because I don't want any man who's going to jump the fence the second he sees the neighbor's greener grass.'"

Carter let out a low whistle. He could imagine his feisty mother doing exactly that. "Can't say I blame her, Dad. You did dump her for Valerie."

"After two dates with Valerie, I knew she wasn't the one," Roger said. Across the street, Mayor Paxton emerged from the barber shop. He gave Roger and Carter a wave, calling out a quick hello. Roger echoed the greeting.

Carter nodded in return. "So, what was it about Valerie that told you she was the wrong one?"

"She was too easy—and I don't mean that just in the bedroom department—but overall, she chased me, she catered to me, and then treated me like a little trophy to remember her summer by. That's nice, but only on a temporary basis. Your mother, well, she had standards. And by golly, when I didn't meet them, she washed her hands of me."

"A challenge, huh?" That was what Lauren was, for sure. She always had been. And way out of his league—smart, beautiful, talented, and elusive as hell.

"Yup. She made me work for it when I went back to her." His father shook his head and chuckled. "I apologized up and down. Told her that if she just took me back I promised I wouldn't jump the fence again. She wasn't buying it, though. Kept on dating Hank. And I knew if I wanted her back, I was going to have to do something drastic."

Carter thought back to the stories he'd heard about his parents' quick courtship and marriage. He'd never realized the why behind the story, but hearing it now, he wondered if he might have done the same thing if he'd been in his father's shoes. "Something drastic...like propose?"

Roger nodded. "I had a little savings, but I used it all to go buy her a ring. I knew if I didn't marry her, some other guy was gonna be smarter and faster and scoop her up, and I'd lose my chance forever. The diamond was so small you needed a magnifying glass to see it, but your mother didn't care. She burst out crying when I dropped down on one knee and asked her to marry me, right there." Roger pointed across the street. "When I knew she was the one, I didn't care if the whole town saw me telling her how much I loved her. She said yes, and we got married just as summer began to edge into fall. Most beautiful damned wedding ever, with the most beautiful bride ever."

Carter's throat clogged. Every time he heard his father speak about his mother, or vice versa, the love between them came through loud and clear. Their marriage, filled with love and laughter and an ease that others envied, had been the standard Carter used to measure all relationships. And except for a couple of months when he was eighteen, he'd never found another woman who could match that expectation. The woman he'd been engaged to when he lived in Chicago had been driven by her career, not by love for him.

Was that who Lauren was now? Every time he thought he caught a glimpse of the woman he used to know, she retreated behind her career again. Why? Had she changed that much or was something more driving her these days?

"Our road hasn't been easy," Roger went on. "When your mother and I first bought this store, we damned near went broke. It was a tough economy, we had this massive loan for the building, and your mom had just had you. The odds were against us. But we stuck together, because that's what you do when the love is more important than the dollars. You find a way, Carter, if you want to badly enough."

Carter had been so captivated by his father's story that he'd forgotten the ice cream. The last chunk of it fell off the wooden popsicle stick, hit the cement, and was soon swarmed by ants hurrying toward the unexpected treat. "That only works if the other person wants you, too, Dad. And after today, I'm not so sure that's the case."

"Do you love her?" his father asked.

Carter sat back against the hard bench. "Love, well, that's a pretty loaded word. I mean, I used to, and I could again, but—"

"Quit butting and hemming and hawing your way around this. Life is short, son. Take the risk. Love the girl. Say the words. Otherwise, you'll be here next weekend and the weekend after that, and all the weekends to come, wondering what if." Roger got to his feet, then put a hand on Carter's shoulder. "I've never seen you as happy as you were that summer. I know you almost married that one girl in Chicago, but I never saw you smile with her the way you did with Lauren. If you ask me, Lauren was good for you back then, and even though I don't know her that well, it's always been clear she makes you happy. Don't let something that rare get away without giving it your best shot."

Maybe his father was right. Maybe Carter should take a

chance again with Lauren. She was here in town for a few more days, and he'd be a fool to let her leave without one more shot. "I don't think she wants a life in Paradise Key, though. And I'm not leaving. Not after…"

Roger's eyes misted. Any mention of the heart attack and those scary months made his stoic father emotional. "She once did, right? Then all you have to do is remind her why Paradise Key is the perfect place to settle down."

Sort of a marketing campaign for the town—but directed toward one consumer. Maybe an impossible task, but an interesting idea. "Thanks, Dad."

"Anytime, son."

Just as the two of them headed back into the store, Tyson Braddock came striding in. Carter had never really liked the brash, demanding commissioner, but he got along with Roger and frequented the store whenever Carter's father was working. "Afternoon, gentlemen."

"How are you, Tyson?"

"Good, good, Roger. I need to come by next week and get a new fishing rod. Assuming I can get enough time off to fish." Tyson chuckled. "Speaking of being busy, Carter, you might have a lot on your plate soon."

Carter straightened some askew candy bars on the rack by the register. "Me? Why?"

"I met with that Lauren Webster today. She's got some great ideas for bringing this town into the twenty-first century for tourism. I told her to get me a formal proposal, and I'll squeeze some money out of that cheap tourism board. I know Eloise thinks you're the best thing since sliced bread, so I think you should talk to her and get her on board. Tourism is going to boom in this town, I tell you. Boom. I see ads in airports and magazines, and before you know it, Paradise Key will be so overrun with tourists we'll be drowning in money. We're talking contests, prizes, stuffed animals, bright T-shirts, hell, maybe even a mascot. Something memorable, like a mermaid. They have those mermaids up in Weeki-Wachi, and that's done wonders for that little town. I told Lauren I want a mermaid here. Hell, maybe even a merman. Whatever it takes to get people talking about our little corner of the world."

Mermaids? T-shirts? Mascots? What the hell? *Trust me*, Lauren had said. She'd told him she understood what this small town meant to him, to its residents. She'd given him that story about her father, made him care about her again, made him believe her. And now she'd gone and created some huge marketing campaign with Tyson that was bound to change the very fabric of Paradise Key. Take the small town he loved so much and make it a kitschy, tacky commercial. Doing everything she had sworn she would never do. Lauren had changed—and not in the ways he'd thought.

"You look like your best friend ran off with your dog," Tyson said to Carter. "Cheer up. This is good news. We'll finally make this town into something."

"It already was something, Tyson." Carter scowled. "It doesn't need to be anything other than that."

Chapter Eight

"**D**OUBLE SCOOP CHOCOLATE with hot fudge, marshmallow, and peanut butter sauce."

Sofia let out a low whistle at Lauren's order. "PMS or a bad day?"

They were standing inside the Delicious Scoops ice cream parlor, a shop close to Jenna's business. Lauren had stopped in earlier to say hello to her friend, but Jenna was crazy busy with work, and Lauren promised to catch up later. She'd had a glimpse of Zach, Jenna's boyfriend, and couldn't miss the obvious sparks between them. It had both made her envious and reminded her of Carter.

Hence the need for chocolate. Lots of it.

"Bad day. Carter. Work. Life. The trifecta of stress," Lauren said. Across the counter, the perky girl who worked at the ice cream shop was bustling between the freezer and the massive pumps that held the flavored toppings. Lauren nodded to the addition of whipped cream and a cherry. Might as well go all in and do it right. Enough sugar might take the edge off the panic lingering under the surface of her thoughts. "After this, I'll take you up on the offer of grabbing a rum and coke at the bar. Maybe all of that will be enough."

"Enough for what?"

Lauren took the dish of ice cream from the young girl, thanked her, and tossed a tip into the glass jar, then led the way to a small table outside. Sofia had agreed to meet Lauren here at the end of the day, so they could catch up. After the time at the beach with Carter and the afternoon meeting with Tyson Braddock, Lauren could use some bourbon on her ice cream. "Enough to forget my job is hanging by a thread, but I might have saved it by going against a promise I made, and that things between Carter and me aren't as over as I thought they were."

Sofia laughed. "Since when did you think they were over? I've known you for years, Lauren, and you never stopped caring about that guy."

"Of course I did. I married someone else." Lauren took a bite of the ice cream. The chocolate glided along her tongue, cool and sweet. Perfect.

Sofia arched a brow. "And that's evidence you forgot about Carter? Because you fell in love with someone else?"

Had Lauren ever really been in love with the man she had married? Their courtship and marriage had all been practical, as if the two of them were following steps laid before them. They'd both worked in marketing, and had met when their two firms had allied to work on a massive project for the city of New York. Her father had approved of the match, telling her that Aaron was the perfect man for her.

She'd never had that swept-off-her-feet heady feeling she'd had that summer with Carter. She'd never tumbled to the sand in a fevered desire to have her ex-husband, the way she had with Carter. "What I had with Carter was wild, irresponsible."

Sofia laughed. "And what's wrong with that? I think a little wild is a good thing."

That was because fiery Sofia personified a little wild. All of Lauren's friends, in fact, were far more carefree than Lauren had ever been, except for that one summer. And she had paid for that many times over, with a father who stopped speaking to her and a mother who had never looked at her daughter the same way again. "Maybe when you're eighteen, but I'm almost thirty. I have a career and a rent payment and—"

Sofia mocked a yawn. "And that is exactly why you need a little wild and irresponsible in your life. When was the last time you had either?"

"Uh…today." Lauren pushed the half-eaten ice cream to the side. "Carter and I were alone on the beach and things got a little…close. I almost made a huge mistake."

"Did you sleep with him?" Sofia leaned forward. "Do tell, because right now, my life is more boring than the stock market pages of the *Wall Street Journal*."

"No. I didn't sleep with him. Worse." Lauren sighed. "I almost fell for him again. When I realized that I was in over my head, I told him I had to go, and did exactly that. We barely exchanged ten words on the ride home. Now all I have to do is not talk to him the rest of the time I'm in Paradise Key."

And especially not tell him about the deal she had worked out with Tyson. It involved the exact kind of marketing that Carter didn't want—big and broad and touting Paradise Key as a vacation destination. Of course, she was going to have to do it on a ridiculously small budget, but she'd worked with less before. In the meeting this afternoon, every time she'd tried to steer Tyson toward something tamer, he'd nixed it. He promised her that without the support of the commissioners, it didn't matter what the tourism board decided. "The dollars start and stop with the commissioners," he said. "So if I'm on board, that's all you need."

Tyson wanted to hire McNally and Webster, and had even offered to bring in the rest of the commissioners and the tourism board that afternoon to get some ink on a contract so she could get started right away. The problem? It was everything she had promised Carter she wouldn't do. So she'd hesitated on executing the contract, on making this a done deal.

"Self-protection by avoiding and over-indulging in sugar?" A wry grin crossed Sofia's face. "I get that. I'm dating this guy in Key West. He's a great guy, but he doesn't exactly make me want to run off to Vegas and elope or anything. Sometimes, though, there's...safety in not going with the riskier option."

"I agree." Lauren got to her feet and tossed away her trash. Right now, with her career in upheaval, and her life waiting for her back in New York, the last thing she needed was another risk. She'd been crazy to rekindle things with Carter this morning. Crazier still to keep on thinking about the man, but he lingered on the edge of every thought, every word. Damn it. She needed to clear her head, get back on track. The last time she had let herself get distracted by Carter, she'd nearly thrown her entire life away. This time, the stakes were higher. Her father was counting on her not to screw this up.

Okay, so maybe there wasn't enough chocolate for her problems. Or rum and Coke for that matter. The only solution was to go back to New York until she no longer caught the scent of the ocean in the air.

"Want to walk the beach?" she said to Sofia.

"Absolutely." The two of them headed across the street and down to the sandy shore. Lauren kicked off her shoes, and Sofia did the same.

As soon as she sank her toes into the cool, deep sand, Lauren's mind rocketed back to this morning. To the picnic with Carter, the paddleboarding, the moment he'd kissed her, and how much she'd wanted more. Okay, so maybe walking the beach wasn't the smartest way to stop thinking about Carter or to put Paradise Key behind her.

The only thing that would truly cure her was heading

back to the city. Get caught in the hustle and bustle and the noises. But she couldn't do that until she had a contract in hand. Tyson had agreed verbally, but she still needed the entire commission and tourism board aligned with the plan, to be sure it would be a success. She almost had what she wanted—Tyson had assured her the deal was as good as done—so why did she feel so terrible? "Can I ask your advice?"

"Sure," Sofia said.

"I'm working with Tyson to convince Paradise Key to hire my firm to do their tourism marketing. But this place is steeped in small-town thinking. They don't seem to want to expand or God forbid, bring in 'big city' ideas. Tyson agrees with me—well, more or less because he's advocating an approach I think is a bit tacky—and although we have a tentative plan in place, I still have to sell the rest of the commission on it before I get the contract in place. You run into the same thing in Key West, I'm sure."

"Definitely. The Keys are essentially just a lot of small towns, except with awesome weather and snorkeling." She grinned. "I'm thinking of buying the Paradise Key Resort, and I'm running into the same brick walls, so I feel your pain."

"Really? That's awesome. You'd be perfect to renovate and run the resort. I might even have to come back and stay here in the winter. Just to give you some market research and customer input." Lauren laughed.

"If I get it, I'll always have room for you." Sofia bent down, picked up a shell, then skimmed it across the ocean. It sank to the bottom with a tiny plop. "Paradise Key is all about relationships. Most of the locals have been here forever, and unless you live here, they see you as an outsider. To me, that's the key to getting an in with the commission and the tourism board."

That made sense. She thought of Eloise's rescinded brownies/blondies. "How can I build a relationship with all those people in a few days, though?"

"How did you build one—or rather, almost build one—with Carter in a few hours?" Sofia arched a brow. "You got personal."

Lauren thought of how close she and Carter had come to sleeping together earlier. Even when they were young, their relationship had gone from zero to sixty almost overnight. "More than personal."

Sofia laughed. "Well, I'm not suggesting you do *that* with anyone on the tourism board. But to me, the key to getting personal is finding something that connects you to the other person. Those people just want to know that you care about their town as much as they do. That your big-city firm will treat it with small-town gloves."

Lauren mulled over Sofia's words for a little while, as the tide slowly came in with the end of the day and the beach emptied out. "That's great advice, actually. I think I have some ideas on how to do that." A way to combine what

Tyson wanted with what Carter and Eloise wanted. A marriage of sorts, between tacky and true.

"You can start right now, by the way, with one of the town's sexiest residents." Sofia gave Lauren a mischievous grin, then nodded in the direction of a figure coming toward them on the beach. A tall, muscular figure that Lauren recognized. "Whoops, would you look at the time? I better go. I have…a thing."

"Sofia, don't—"

"Leave you alone with a man you still care about?" Sofia's grin widened. "Why would I do such a thing? Unless it was for your own good." Before Lauren could stop her, Sofia waved goodbye and headed back toward her shoes.

CARTER HAD SPENT the latter half of the afternoon working the store and stewing about what Tyson had told him. He'd debated going to Eloise and Merle, but they had already left for the day when he stopped by the town hall. Then he'd seen Lauren's car, and caught a glimpse of her heading down to the beach with Sofia.

"Hey, Carter." Sofia gave him a wink as she passed by in the opposite direction. "It sure is a nice night for romance."

"You wouldn't be saying that as a hint, would you?" Sofia's breath was wasted if so, because Carter had no intentions of falling under Lauren's spell again. *Trust me.*

That had been his first mistake.

"Me, hinting at romance? Never." Sofia's smile widened, then she waved and loped back toward the parking lot.

Twenty feet away, Lauren had stopped walking. She stood at the edge of the water, while the incoming tide brushed her toes and rushed out again. A few people walked along the beach, couples mostly, kissing beneath the soft light of the moon, their voices light and happy.

He came up beside Lauren and faced the endless ocean, stretching in a dark blanket to the edge of the earth. "Nice night."

"It is."

Now that he was here, he wasn't quite sure what to say. He'd had a whole irate speech prepared earlier, but it went out of his head the second he saw the graceful curve of her neck and the wide beauty of her eyes sparkling under the stars. "I heard you talked to Tyson."

"I did. He's really excited about the—"

"What you sold to him is the exact opposite of what you told me you wanted to do. I was starting to get on board, then you used my name to switch it to some joke of a marketing campaign. Contests? Stuffed animals? Paradise Key branded bikinis? Really?"

"Those were Tyson's ideas, but I—"

But he didn't hear her protests. All he saw was a woman he thought he knew, who had changed far more than he'd realized until this afternoon. "I thought you knew this town.

I thought you knew me. You don't know either." He took a step closer. "And I don't know you."

She bristled, and her green eyes went cold. "I'm doing my job."

Her job. Yeah, looking at the bottom line instead of the people involved. Had Lauren drank that much of the corporate Kool-Aid in the years since he'd met her, that she would try to sell Paradise Key like it was some new toy at a fast food restaurant? "You want to know what sells this town? What makes it an amazing place to live in and visit?"

"Small-town values, neighbors helping each other, yada yada." She threw up her hands. "I get that, Carter. And I'm going to make sure the marketing campaign reflects that, regardless of what Tyson thinks. Why don't you believe me about that?"

He shook his head. She might as well have been reciting a script. He'd heard Tyson loud and clear today, and Tyson had been convinced Lauren was planning one of those hideous marketing campaigns that would turn this sleepy little town into a joke. All she was doing right now was covering her tracks so that Carter would throw his support behind the plan.

He used to think he knew her. That she loved Paradise Key as much as he did. But the way she'd circumvented everything they had talked about…

Trust me. He'd done that and nearly made a mistake of epic proportions. "Tomorrow morning at eight, be at my father's store," Carter said. If he couldn't get Lauren to see his point of view, maybe he could change her mind by making it personal. Only to protect the town from some kids' toy in a hot-dog meal insane sales pitch. "You'll get that inside peek at Paradise Key that you always wanted. And you'll get plenty of time to sell Eloise and everyone else on your plan."

Or spend enough time with them to make it clear to Lauren that her kitschy marketing ideas weren't welcome in Paradise Key. The idea hadn't occurred to him until just that second. If he wanted a way to show Lauren the true heart of Paradise Key, there was no better opportunity than tomorrow morning.

"What are you talking about?"

"You'll find out tomorrow. Think of it as a surprise." Not the kind that involved a paddleboard and a secluded beach, but one that would serve Carter's purposes much better. In the years since he had returned to Paradise Key and seen how his father supported this town, and how that town rallied around its people, he'd become Paradise Key's biggest advocate. Hence the work with the tourism board, and the project he had going tomorrow.

"Eight sharp, Lauren," he said, before she could object. Then he turned on his heel and went back to the parking lot.

Sofia had been right. It was a nice night. Just not for romance.

Chapter Nine

THE SOUND OF hammers hitting nails reached Lauren before she got to Malone's Market. It was a clear day, a bright and warm Saturday, and downtown Paradise Key was already starting to get busy. To the back of the market, there was hum of voices, the soft sound of a radio playing pop tunes, and the steady beat of hammers.

And on a ladder, Carter himself, a toolbelt slung low on his hips. He caught sight of Lauren, gave her a wave, then climbed down and crossed to her. "Hey, you came."

"I said I would. But I thought we were having a meeting at your dad's store." She glanced around. "It looks like half the town is here."

"Half the town *is* here." He grinned. "Helping one of their own. You wanted to know that the real Paradise Key is like? Well, this is it." He waved toward the people. "One of our own is in trouble, so we came together to help."

"One of your own?"

Carter gestured toward a petite blonde woman in a pair of paint-stained overalls. She was talking to Carter's father and two other men. "Lynette Halliwell has hit some hard times lately. Lost her husband last year, and then the store they run got damaged in a storm. She let the insurance policy lapse, and she had no money to fix the place. My dad organized a party to help her. And here we are."

Lauren thought of the neighborhood she lived in, the coldness of her neighbors. She couldn't name more than a handful of them, if that many. When the summer caused rolling blackouts or winter storms shut down the city, New Yorkers stayed in their apartments behind doormen and locked lobbies. She couldn't imagine something like this ever happening where she lived. A part of her envied Lynette, which was crazy. The woman had gone through some serious hard times, but she clearly had friends and people who loved her enough to donate an entire Saturday to helping her get back on her feet.

"That's really nice," Lauren said. Though nice wasn't a strong enough word for what she saw around her. People laughing, helping each other, pouring ice water, handing out materials—this was a true community effort, coupled with a lighthearted mood and cheery attitudes.

"If you want to know what makes Paradise Key special," Carter said, reaching for a smaller tool belt on the makeshift table beside him, "you gotta get your hands dirty."

"What? Me? But I can't—"

"Get outside your comfort zone, Lauren Webster." Before she could protest, he draped the tool belt around her waist and fastened it. Then he handed her a hammer and a pile of nails, and walked away, whistling as he did.

She thought of leaving, but then she looked around her—at Eloise, Delilah, even Merle who was upright for once, and a lot of other residents of Paradise Key she didn't know, and remembered Sofia's words about how to sell the town on her ideas—get personal. What better way to get personal than by sweating in the sun and fixing up a dress shop?

She crossed to Carter's father, who was cutting the siding on a miter saw before handing the pieces to a waiting volunteer. "How can I help, Mr. Malone?"

"Lauren. So nice to see you again." He nodded toward the next piece of white wood. "Hold that in place while I measure and cut it. And if you don't mind being my eyes, can you doublecheck to make sure I get my measurements right before I cut? They make the numbers on those measuring tapes smaller every year."

She laughed. She'd always liked Roger when she'd seen him, on the few times she'd met Carter at the store over that summer. Lauren did as he asked, checking the tape and calling out the measurements as he made them, holding the long boards steady as he cut, then handing each piece off to a waiting volunteer. "It's really nice of the town to do this for Lynette."

"We pick a project every month," Roger said. "Plenty of people here need help, whether it's to paint their house or repair a swing or just get the lawn mowed in a time when the family is overwhelmed."

"We?"

Roger nodded. "Carter and me. It was all his idea, actually. After I had my heart attack, folks showed up at the house with food, offers to help with the store and the yard work. You name it, someone was there to help us with it. This town really came together, went all out for me and my wife, and all I had was a little heart trouble."

A little heart trouble had been a brush with death, according to Carter, but Roger wasn't the kind of guy to ask for attention or sympathy. Never had Lauren seen something like that—a whole town banding together to support one resident. She'd once had the flu and no one even noticed she hadn't left her apartment in a week, never mind dropped off a casserole. Of course, the flu wasn't a heart attack or the passing of a spouse, but still, she couldn't imagine the same thing happening in New York. "This place really is special, isn't it?"

"More than you know." Roger's gaze took in the neighbors surrounding them, and his eyes misted a little. He shook his head, cleared his throat, then got back to work.

Lauren worked beside Roger for an hour, whittling the pile of siding down one piece at a time. As he worked, he stayed on neutral topics, like how long Lynette's store had been in Paradise Key, what shop had been in that space before hers, how the town had changed over the years, and what was planned for the empty lot on 4th Street.

The entire time, every inch of Lauren stayed attuned to

Carter. He moved from project to project, helping wherever he was needed, giving direction, or sometimes just offering encouragement. Everyone who talked to him seemed to love him.

Lauren could see why. He was handsome but likeable, friendly, and approachable. He took a genuine interest in the people around him. He knew everyone's name, remembered their kids' names, where they worked, and where they'd spent their last vacation. Carter had been amazing when he was young, but he'd grown up into the kind of man that most women dreamed of meeting.

The customer she'd seen in the store—Jacob something—came by with a short elderly woman on his arm, followed by Heidi, the waitress. Carter put down his hammer to talk to them.

Lauren nearly dropped the board in her hands. Heidi sauntered over to Carter with a can of soda. He thanked her, took a long sip, then went back to work. Heidi scowled as she got back in her car and left. The flicker of jealousy in Lauren's chest went away as the buxom waitress did.

"There's the last piece." Roger handed it off to the young boy who had been running between the building and the makeshift workbench, then shut the miter saw off. Roger wiped the sawdust off his jeans and out of his hair before grabbing two icy water bottles and handing one to Lauren. "Thanks for your help."

"You're welcome." It had been more fun than she'd expected. And she'd learned a lot about measuring wood, cutting angles, and installing siding, along with the history of almost every business in Paradise Key.

"You know, he always loved you." When Lauren gave Roger a questioning glance, he raised his water bottle in Carter's direction. "You were all he talked about that summer, every single time he came to work or sat down at the dinner table. After you two broke up, though, he never, ever talked about you."

"And that's how you know he always loved me?" She scoffed. "Sounds like the opposite."

"Carter's a lot more like me than he thinks." Roger started crossing the small lawn, stopping to beckon for Lauren to follow him. He opened a can of paint and began to stir it with a wooden stick. "When he deeply cares, he goes quiet. He buries himself in some project or work, and clams right up. But ever since you came back to town, it's like a valve has been opened. You're all he talks about again."

The thought of Carter talking about her made Lauren happier than she expected. He hadn't broken up with her and moved on, forgetting all about their summer romance. And he'd been telling the truth when he said he wanted more than just a one-night stand.

But she wasn't staying in Paradise Key. Sure, if she landed the account, she could come back a few times a year. They couldn't build a relationship on a handful of weekends. What did he expect? That she'd uproot her life in New York and settle down here, with the sand and the surf and the locals who were lending a helping hand?

That actually sounded like a really nice way to live. But she had made a promise to her father, and there was no way Lauren was going to break that.

"Oh, there's Marla." Roger's face lit at the sight of his wife. "I'm going to go help her set up for lunch." He closed the paint can again, and set it to the side. Then he crossed to her, took the petite brunette in his arms, and kissed her. She laughed and gazed up at her husband, her eyes full of adoration and love.

The scene was so intimate, so sweet, that Lauren had to look away. Her parents had never behaved like that, not that Lauren could remember, and she'd never looked at her ex-husband with that kind of love. She'd never seen him light up when she walked into a room, and never rushed off to be with him.

There was only one man she had rushed to be with. Only one man who had made her heart light up when she saw him.

Her gaze went to Carter, who was now helping his parents with the lunch preparations. He caught her eye, and for a long second, the connection held. Then he dipped his head and went back to setting out platters of sandwiches, and the moment was over before it began.

HIS FATHER AND mother were conspiring. Carter watched them talking, their heads close together, as they finished setting up a trio of picnic tables for lunch. "What are you two concocting over there?"

"Nothing." His mother smiled slyly and put a hand on her husband's arm. "We were just thinking it might be nice if you and Lauren sat together at lunch."

"What is this, sixth grade?" He scowled. "I don't need my parents to fix me up with a lunch buddy."

"You do if you want to save her from everyone's favorite commissioner." His father nodded toward the street. Tyson Braddock was getting out of a car, then striding toward the worksite. Clearly not here to volunteer, given his suit and shiny shoes.

Aggravation swelled inside Carter. Tyson and his ideas— the opposite of what this town needed. One look at the group who had assembled to help Lynette would tell any reasonable person that Paradise Key wasn't some tawdry place for party animals. It was a community, a home, a haven.

Lauren had essentially sold out the town. She'd gone with Tyson's tacky ideas instead of capturing the true essence of Paradise Key. The promises she had made on the beach had been gone the minute Tyson Braddock put some money on the table. Carter should have known better than to think he knew what kind of adult Lauren would become. He'd met her when he was eighteen, only known her for a few months.

What he thought he saw in her eyes this week hadn't been the truth at all.

Lauren put down the pitcher of lemonade in her hands, then crossed to Tyson. The two of them chatted amiably, like old friends, and the aggravation in Carter's chest multiplied. He grabbed a plate of food before dropping onto the wooden picnic bench. His mother cast him a look and tilted her head in Lauren's direction, but Carter just hunched over his meal. The turkey sandwich could have been cardboard for all he tasted it.

He'd hoped that having her volunteer at the rebuilding party for Lynette would make Lauren see what a great town Paradise Key was. That she shouldn't become a sellout just to get a contract for her father. What had happened to the Lauren he knew? The rebel who wanted more out of life than the rigid career-driven world of her father? When had her career become more important than the people around her?

Lauren said goodbye to Tyson, and headed to the food. She assembled a plate for herself, but before she could find a seat, Carter's mother stepped in. "Here, come sit with us," she said, guiding Lauren by the elbow to the space across from Carter. "It's been so long since we've seen you, Lauren."

Carter's mother was one of those women everyone wished they had as a mother. She baked cookies, had dinner ready every night at six, and had been a hands-on mom with Carter, going to all his baseball games and attending every school play. He loved her fiercely. Just not right this second. "I'm done eating," he said, then got to his feet and tossed the rest of his sandwich in the trash.

Chapter Ten

LAUREN WENT BACK to her room at the Airbnb late in the afternoon, hot and sweaty, her arms and legs aching in a way they never did in Pilates class. She took a long shower, then opened her laptop to start working on the proposal for Tyson. He'd told her he'd talked to the other commissioners. If she could come up with something that really wowed them, they'd be on board.

The problem? Tyson's version of *wow* was the antithesis of everything Lauren had tried to do in her career. When she'd talked to him today, she'd tried again to sway him toward the idea she had shared with Carter, but Tyson cut her off mid-sentence. *I want Paradise Key to be a city people talk about. Nobody's going to talk about us and yoga on the beach.*

Lauren spent a solid half hour trying to write the proposal. Every time she started typing, though, nothing felt right. No words flowed from her mind to the screen. She deleted, typed, deleted again. Finally, a little after six, she gave up and closed the lid on the laptop.

She needed a second opinion. Someone who worked in her industry and could maybe put this in perspective. And work on a limited budget, because Lauren had a feeling if she wanted to convince Tyson—and her father—to go with something more befitting her image of Paradise Key, she'd have to do it on her own dime.

Evie picked up on the first ring. "Hey! I was just running out."

"That's fine. I really was calling to ask a favor." Lauren opened the window of her room to let in the cool night breeze. "I'm trying to land the Paradise Key marketing account, and I have to go through Tyson Braddock to get the other commissioners and the tourism board to sign off. The problem is, Tyson wants one of those flashy, tacky approaches, as if Paradise Key can be the next Vegas."

"Eww. That's totally not right for this town."

"I know, I agree." She sat on the bed and leaned against the pillows. "You're in broadcasting, you're gorgeous, and you know this town. Could I hire you to do a little publicity for Paradise Key? Sort of show them what I mean? I have a feeling Tyson isn't going to agree with me unless he sees my ideas in action."

"Sure. That sounds like a great idea. Maybe we could do a video series. A sort of *get to know the town* thing."

Lauren jotted *videos* down on her notepad. "I love that. I think it would work wonderfully, especially with you on the videos." They spent a few minutes talking through some ideas. Evie had a lot of on-camera experience and would undoubtedly give the videos a professional feel, coupled with her approachable style. Lauren could already see the possibilities in her mind.

It wasn't Greyhound, but it was a start. For the first time in a long time, Lauren was excited about her job. If she could execute this and everyone could see her vision for Paradise Key, then this might just be a project she felt proud of at the end of the day. And one that would finally show her father she could succeed in this job.

"I'm excited you're doing this," Evie said. "Publicizing Paradise Key. I think it's a great place to visit, and it would be nice to see more people grow to love it like Lily did."

Lauren sobered. "She did love this place, didn't she? I think she loved it more than any of us."

"It was her spirit. She never did anything halfway." Evie sighed. "Life is short, Lauren. We need to live it more."

She glanced down at her notepad, thinking about the work she still had to do on the campaign, as well as convincing her father to try a different approach. "It's tough to do all that when you have bills to pay and people counting on you."

"The people counting on you are also the people who want you to experience life, Lauren. That's one thing Lily did, and something the rest of us need to learn to do. If only to honor her memory." Evie sighed again, then brightened. "Anyway, I have to go. Let's try and grab some drinks later this week, okay?"

"Sure. Thanks for the help. And the listening ear." Lauren hung up with Evie, then texted the rest of them but all the girls had plans for the evening, so she walked down to Scallywag's alone. It was a beautiful, clear night full of stars and a crescent moon. Inside, the bar was quiet, with only a handful of customers and the same female bartender behind the bar. Had that only been less than a week ago? It felt like a lifetime. Lauren selected a stool and ordered a glass of wine.

At the end of the bar, the same rotund man who had been there the first night was finishing off a beer. Delilah, the bartender, took his empty glass and put it in a bucket of soapy water under the bar. "Need another, Nelson?"

"Maybe just one," the man said. His words slurred a bit. He fished a few dollars out of his pocket, then put them on the bar. Delilah exchanged them for a beer.

"You have a ride home tonight?"

Nelson shrugged. "I dunno. Might walk."

"We can't have that." Delilah gave him a kind smile, then waved toward a heavyset man wearing a ballcap and playing darts. "Hey, Joey. Think you can give Nelson a ride home?"

"Sure thing," the other man called back. "I think it's my turn anyway."

Nelson waved at Joey, giving him a smile. "Thanks, buddy."

"Anytime." Joey finished his dart game, clapped his friend on the shoulder, then collected Nelson from the end of the bar. The two men walked out of Scallywag's, Joey keeping a careful arm around Nelson's shoulder and nodding appreciatively as Nelson recounted a weepy tale about his ex-wife.

When they were gone, Delilah washed the empty glasses and set them on a rack to dry. The bar was quiet save for a few couples lingering at the tables. Country music played on the sound system, providing a steady beat for the conversations around the room.

"What did Joey mean by it being his turn?" Lauren asked.

Delilah shrugged. "Oh, we all take turns watching out for Nelson. He's a great guy who has had a lot of heartbreak in his life. He doesn't much like talking about it or dealing with it, so he comes here, and someone always makes sure he gets home okay."

Once again, Lauren thought of New York. She had a better chance of being robbed and left for dead in an alley than having a stranger give her a ride home. Of course, New York had taxis and subways and buses—options outside of strangers. But still, when it came to *love thy neighbor*, Paradise Key seemed to take that commandment seriously. "That's really great."

Delilah smiled. "It's what keeps me in this town. The weather's amazing, but all the sunshine in the world can't make up for mean people. Paradise Key truly is paradise, and for all the right reasons."

"I'm beginning to see that." Lauren fiddled with the

cocktail napkin underneath her wineglass, thinking about the proposal she'd been trying to write, and why she hadn't been able to put anything together. *Paradise Key truly is paradise, and for all the right reasons.*

Lauren straightened and gestured toward the bartender. "Hey, Delilah, do you have a pen?"

"Sure, hon." Delilah handed Lauren a pen. "Want a refill, too?"

Lauren nodded, but she'd already begun writing on the cocktail napkin and forgot about the drink as soon as Delilah put it before her. She sketched out the idea she'd shared with Carter, but began to expand upon what she'd said. She drew a city in the background, the stressed woman thinking about carpool and work and dinner, then switching to the beach in Paradise Key, where her mind was blank, the smile on her face wide. Beneath that, a slogan. *A true paradise...for all the right reasons.*

That was it. The slogan she'd been searching for. From there, she could hang the entire campaign. She knew she had the perfect idea, knew it in a deep, visceral way. This was the campaign that would market Paradise Key, but to the kind of people who were seeking a true home away from home.

Lauren laid a generous tip on the bar beside her still-full wineglass. "Thank you, Delilah. You just gave me the best idea I've had in months."

"You're welcome, hon." She took the money and started cashing out Lauren's bill. "You make sure to come back, you hear?"

"Oh, I'll be back to Paradise Key," Lauren said. "I guarantee it." She gathered up her napkin, then turned to go.

Just then, the door to Scallywag's opened and Carter stepped in. Lauren's heart skipped a beat. His stoic face didn't say happy to see her—and she couldn't blame him, not after what had happened with the day on the beach and the meeting with Tyson. After today, she understood Carter's alliance to Paradise Key, and realized why he had fought so hard against Tyson's ideas.

Now she had something she thought would work on all fronts. She'd sold herself on her idea—now she had to convince someone else that her motives were true.

CARTER HAD TOLD himself he was going to give Lauren space. That she'd made her choice by aligning with Tyson Braddock and trying to change her mind was an exercise in futility. Then he'd talked to his parents, and heard how much she'd helped today. How interested she'd been in the town, and how much she seemed to care.

Could he have read her wrong? Could it be that Tyson was bragging about something that hadn't really happened? And maybe Carter was being, as his mother had called him, a stubborn fool who needed to get his head out of his emotions. It wouldn't be the first time he'd let his head make decisions for his heart.

When he walked into Scallywag's and saw Lauren, his breath caught. She was sitting there on the bar stool, turned toward him, dressed in a pair of khaki shorts, a dark blue tank top, and a pair of white sneakers. Her long hair was down around her shoulders, freed from that morning's ponytail. She looked...amazing. Approachable. Like the woman he had once fallen in love with.

Truth be told, ever since the conversation with his father, he hadn't been able to put her out of his mind—or the fact that life had an expiration date, a reminder that came in light of Lily's sudden and unexpected death just a few years after Carter's father had nearly died. Every time Carter thought about those dark months, he saw his mother, and the emptiness that filled her eyes as she contemplated a life without the man she loved more than anything.

His parents had always been a team, even when the economy put the squeeze on their finances or a tropical storm wiped out the store's supplies. They had surely worried and stressed, but Carter had never seen them argue or fret. He'd thought that was because running the store was easy and dull—until he'd actually been the one behind the register and realized how many millions of small decisions went into every sale, and how one wrong decision could domino financially.

Throughout it all, his parents had remained steadfast in their love for each other. Carter envied them that love, that connection, and in the last few weeks as he passed his thirtieth birthday and saw most of his friends married and settled down, realized he wanted the same thing in his life.

He nodded toward Delilah, waving off her offer of a beer. Instead, he beelined for the only woman he noticed in the room. "Hi, Lauren."

"I was just leaving," she said. "So you can spare me the lecture about the marketing campaign. I have another idea that I think will work better, and I'd appreciate it if you would hear me out."

He held up his hands in a *whoa-peace* gesture. "I wasn't going to lecture you, and I wasn't going to talk about the marketing campaign, at least not right this second. I was going to ask you to take a walk with me. It's a beautiful night and I'd like to spend it with you, Lauren."

Her eyes widened with surprise. "All right. I'm heading back to my room. You can walk with me if you'd like."

"I would. Very much." They walked out of the bar, and turned left. The air was still warm, the stars above bright. The town itself had mostly shut down for the night, and the streets were quiet. He could hear the ocean off to the left, and the occasional sound of a car heading somewhere. In the dark, everything about Paradise Key seemed mysterious, like the town was hiding behind a curtain, waiting for daybreak to reveal its true beauty.

Carter fell into step beside Lauren, an easy cadence that made it seem like they had been together for decades.

Whenever he had been with her, there was no hesitation in conversation or connection. From the first day, it had seemed as if they were meant to be together. Except for now. A palpable wall of iciness stood between them, a wall he blamed on himself.

"Thank you for your help today," he said. Okay, so that wasn't exactly breaking down the barrier between them, but it was a start.

"It was a great day." Lauren brushed her hair back off her shoulders, unaware the simple movement bared them to his view. "I didn't think I'd be much help, but your dad was really patient with me. He said you've been doing this for the people of the town for years. That's wonderful, Carter."

Carter shrugged. "It just seemed like the thing to do after what people did for my dad." He could still remember the piles of casseroles in the freezer, the neighbors who mowed the lawn without being asked, the dozen or so people who stepped up and volunteered to work a shift at the store so Roger wouldn't lose any income while he was in the hospital. All those favors his father had quietly done over the years had been repaid a hundredfold.

Lauren turned to study him. "You've changed. In good ways."

The moon danced in her eyes, and he ached to take her hands in his. To draw Lauren to his chest and never let go. But he hesitated, unable to read her tone for notes of indifference or interest. "I don't know about that. I think this is who I was underneath, or who we can all be underneath, given the opportunity. For me, it just took a wake-up call to bring me back to reality. My father and I may not have always gotten along, but coming home after he had his heart attack really opened my eyes to what's important and what doesn't matter."

"Maybe that's what I need. Some kind of wake-up call." She started walking again, her pace slowing the closer they got to the place where she was staying.

She said the words so softly he almost didn't hear her. "What do you mean?"

Lauren shrugged. "I was just talking to Evie about this a little while ago. I feel like I've gotten off track in the last couple of years. I married someone I wasn't in love with. Then got divorced and felt like a failure. Ended up screwing up a big account and costing my father millions. And I'm working a job that I honestly don't love."

"Then why not ditch it all?"

"Because I have bills to pay like any other American. I can't just up and dump my life. And I..." She took in a breath. "I can't let my father down. He needs me now."

"If I remember right, he was never there when you need-ed him." They were harsh words, and for a second, Carter wished he could take them back. He knew she loved her father, even if he hadn't been the most demonstrative, or the most loving, parent.

"He was a single parent and running a company and—"

"And you've made excuses for him all your life, Lauren. He's become your way out." The words were out before he could stop them, words that had been inside him since that summer. He'd never realized how angry he was that she had gone back to the very world she said she hated, until just now. Maybe a part of him had hoped she would tell him not to leave Paradise Key, to stay with her and make a life there. But she had taken the breakup with no drama, no pleading words.

Lauren stopped walking. "What are you talking about? I've never used my father as my way out of anything."

"When we broke up, it wasn't all on me, Lauren. Yeah, I told you I didn't want to be tied down and I wanted to see the world—"

"And broke my heart. I stupidly thought you were in love with me."

"I was, Lauren." Now he took her hands in his. She stood there, unyielding and stony. "But then you said it was okay, because you were never really serious about living here. You talked about your father's expectations and college and the life you had laid out before you."

"Are you blaming our breakup on me? Because you were the one who ended it, not me. Can you blame me for going back to the life I had rather than staying here after you made it clear you were leaving without me?"

"Not at all. I made the choices I made. And you made yours." At the time, he'd thought he was heading down the right road. And maybe he had been. If they'd stayed together and she'd given up her life and future for him, would they have ended up happy and satisfied? Or would they have broken up anyway? Seventeen and eighteen was far too young to make a lifetime decision. "But were you ever truly happy after you left here that summer? Because if you were, or if you are now, then say the word and I'll walk away and leave you alone."

She held his gaze for a long time. A couple walked by them, whispering in hushed tones about a trip they'd taken and laughing to themselves. "It's been so long since I was truly happy, Carter, I don't even know how to answer that."

He shifted closer to her. Invading her space. Opening a door he had closed. Overruling his head and letting his heart lead the way. "And when was that last time you *were* truly happy?"

She glanced away. "You know that answer, Carter."

"Do I?" He touched her chin, bringing her gaze back to his. His heart thudded in his chest, and the entire world around him dropped away. All he saw was Lauren's eyes, those deep, green, amazing eyes that grounded him. "When, Lauren?"

"When we were together. That summer...that was the best three months of my life." She broke away from him, shaking her head. "But it was a summer romance. That's not real. That's not how life works. It was temporary. A vacation from reality. Just like this week has been."

"It's only a vacation from reality if you go back." He grinned, lightening the mood because he was afraid if he pushed her too much she would retreat and be lost to him again. Maybe forever. "I thought the life I had in Chicago was my reality, but honestly, it wasn't. I came back here, and I found home. I found people who love one another. A community that supports each other. A place that feels like home every single time I'm here."

She sighed. "That's not what I have. New York City has never felt like home, and my apartment is just a place to sleep."

"Then come back to Paradise Key, Lauren." He wanted to add *come back to me*, but again, he held back instead of pushing her. The last time he'd told her he wanted more than a one-night stand, she had bolted from the beach like the hounds of hell were on her heels. Maybe he had misread her that day, and her interest in him had ended that summer day all those years ago. Carter suspected it hadn't. Lauren was afraid of admitting it, because it would mean changing her life to be with him, regardless of whether they settled down in Paradise Key or in New York. "We can use marketing people here, too. Or if you don't want to do that, then go back to your art and set up a little shop downtown. Life is short—hasn't losing Lily taught you that?"

"Of course it has! But it's not that easy, Carter."

"Why isn't it?" He shifted closer. In the dark, the conversation seemed deeper, more intimate. They were alone on the street, almost as if they were the only ones in the entire world. "Because you're still afraid?"

"I wasn't afraid of anything. You were the one who ran from your life."

"You're right, I did. I thought I was going after what I wanted, but I was wrong. Eighteen isn't the smartest age," he said. "You were brave and a risk-taker when I asked you to paddleboard or jet ski, but when it came to your father, you were the most scared girl I'd ever met. You ran away in the middle of the night. You didn't walk away in broad day-light."

She shook her head. "You don't know my life."

"No. But I do know you. Better than you think." He took her hands again. Held her tight. He had loved her then, he had loved her ever since, and he loved her now. She was a complex, bright, incredible woman who was loyal to a fault. But underneath all of that was a woman who had suffered a great loss when she was young, and that had made her cautious and careful. "I'd hate to see you spend the next ten years unhappy just because you're afraid to take a risk."

"Every time I've taken a risk, it's backfired on me. And hurt my father." She bit her lip, and tears welled in her eyes. "You may not think much of him, but he's all the family I have, Carter. And if I lose him—"

When she cut off the sentence, Carter wanted to take back every word he'd said. Her father was sick, and it was only natural for her to want to protect him and support him.

"I'm sorry, Lauren. I shouldn't have said anything."

"My dad has cancer, Carter. He's not going to get better or go back to his old self. He needs me. He only told me about it because he wants me to take a bigger role in the company. Otherwise, he doesn't talk about it, doesn't tell me how he's feeling. I worry about him a lot, and I want him to know McNally and Webster is in good, capable hands with me. I just have to prove myself with at least one account. I thought Paradise Key would be it."

Carter's heart softened. He knew exactly the worry Lauren was feeling, the helplessness that came with watching from the outside. "Of course it will be. You're brilliant, Lauren. And whatever you want to do with Paradise Key, I'll help you. Maybe we can make the whole T-shirts and stuffed animals thing work."

"That's not how I want to approach it now, regardless of what Tyson Braddock wants. I get what you've said about this town, Carter. I understand so much more after today, with the volunteering for Lynette and watching how Delilah took care of Nelson and made sure he got home okay. This is a home, a place that people love dearly, and it wouldn't be right to sell it as anything other than that. So I'm throwing out Tyson's input and starting over with a different slogan. How does this sound? A true paradise...for all the right reasons."

He loved the idea, and could see it in an advertising campaign, on signs hanging in the stores around town, and even on T-shirts. "That's great! I think it will work perfectly. And best of all, you'll probably have to be here a lot to oversee it."

She shook her head, and disappointment weighed down his smile. "This won't be that kind of job. The budget is small, I can't justify the cost, and my place is with my father. Maybe I can slip in a few trips to Florida here and there, but—"

"You're really going to stay up there?" The hope he'd had that maybe they could try again died inside him. A long-distance relationship was difficult enough, but given how much they worked, it would be downright impossible.

"I have to, Carter. It's where my father is. Where the company is."

He cursed under his breath. "I get that, I do. I moved here to take of my father, so far be it for me to fault you for that. But Lauren, it kills me to think of you living up North, unhappy in your job and your life. That summer, there was joy in your face, your voice. I miss that. I miss you."

She let out a sigh, shaking her head. "What do you want from me, Carter?"

"I want you to be true to you, Lauren. To who you really are." He cupped her jaw, held her gaze with his own. "I want you to be with me. I don't want to lose you. Not again, Lauren."

Tears welled in her eyes. "You're asking something of me that I can't give you, Carter. Not right now."

He had no recourse for that. Giving her a hard time about moving to Paradise Key would be asking her to leave her father. And Carter was the last person on earth to ask anyone to put love ahead of family. "I understand. Maybe we can make this long-distance thing work."

She shook her head again. "I just don't think that's practical. I think..." She drew in a breath, then choked out, "Maybe we should just end it here and now."

For the second time in his life, Carter Malone had lost Lauren Webster. The first time had been because of his own stupidity. His heart broke, and he wished he could rewind to that day on the beach. But he couldn't do that, and couldn't ask her to give up her father for him. This time, he lost her because he loved her enough to let her go. He drew her into his arms, kissed her long and deep, then pulled back, brushed the hair out of her face, and whispered, "I love you."

Then Carter turned and walked into the night, more alone than he'd ever been in his entire life.

Chapter Eleven

LAUREN WATCHED CARTER leave, trying her damnedest to hold back her tears. It was that summer all over again, except she was the one choosing a different path this time. She wanted to run after Carter, tell him she was wrong, they'd figure it out, but then the voice of reason held her in place.

How could she walk away from her father? From what he had asked her to do? After all, she'd been the one to let down the company in the first place, maybe even adding to his stress when he needed to be pouring his energy into fighting the cancer. She needed to be there for him, not just to help run McNally and Webster, but to take care of him, and spend as much time with him as she possibly could. And maybe in the process, they could have the real relationship she'd always wanted. If not, at least she had done her best. He was all the family she had, and no matter what, she would put that first.

As if she had conjured him up, she saw a taxi pull up. Her father emerged from the car, a small bag in one hand. He tipped the driver, then headed up the walkway to the small building where she was staying. "Dad!" Lauren called out. He turned and paused when he saw her. "What are you doing here?"

Gerald Webster put his bag on the stoop, then crossed to his daughter. He was a tall man, with thinning grey hair and piercing blue eyes. He'd lost some weight in the last few months, and the clothes that had once been custom-made for him now ran baggy and loose. In all other respects, no one would know Gerald had been sick. He masked his illness well, and it was only in the late nights at the office that Lauren had seen the toll it was taking on him.

"I'm doing what you should have done." There was no hug, no greeting. As usual, her father was all business, no sentiment. "Landing this account. I've talked to Tyson Braddock and the other commissioners. We worked out a deal, and he's already signed the contract. McNally and Webster will be handling the marketing for this town." He let out a long breath. "I kept hoping you would take care of this."

"I did, and I would have. Once again, you didn't trust me." Lauren fished the cocktail napkin out of her pocket. It irked her that her father had circumvented her, but that was par for the course. He'd rarely trusted her, rarely trusted anybody. His micromanagement had made him very successful, but also almost impossible to work for and reason with. Any other time, Lauren would have backed down and deferred to her father, but not with Paradise Key. The town had grown on her, like a family, in the last few days. "I have a better idea than Tyson does. Something home and hearth, more evocative of what Paradise Key is really like."

Her father waved a dismissive hand without even glancing at the paper. "I know what this town needs."

Carter had been right earlier. For most of her life, Lauren had been afraid to stand up to her father, to step out from his expectations. To tell him the truth. The one time she had fought for what she wanted, she'd ultimately crumbled and messed up the account, maybe out of some misguided self-sabotage. She hadn't loved Greyhound or any of the other accounts she had worked on over the years, but she loved this town, and saw how other people felt about it. People like Roger, Nelson, Delilah, Lynette. She'd met dozens of people in the few days she'd been here, and over the course of that time, begun to see Paradise Key as something other than a revenue stream for the company. She could not stand by and let her father run roughshod over her or this town.

"You have no idea what this town needs, Dad," Lauren said. "You've never spent any real time here."

"What are you talking about? I vacationed here several summers in a row."

"Traveling here and staying in your room all day long making calls isn't being on vacation." She ran a hand through her hair, trying to tamp down her frustration. "All you've ever done is work."

"Because I am committed to the company. I've poured everything I have into that place!" Her father took in a long breath, then everything inside him seemed to shift. He lowered his head. When he spoke again, his voice was lower, sadder. "It's taken me a long time, but I realized on the way down here that you don't have the same commitment to the company that I do."

"I do, Dad. I know I haven't exactly been a rockstar—"

"You don't love it like I do. You never did."

The words hung between them. "I'm trying, Dad. I know how important this is, and with you getting sick…"

He raised his gaze to hers. "I don't want you sitting behind my desk because you feel obligated to do it, Lauren. I want you to be there because you live and breathe this company like I do."

For as long as she could remember, her father had talked about the day she would step into his shoes. Her first day at the company he'd spent telling everyone his daughter was finally working there, and that she was going to be the second-generation leadership. She had stood there while he proudly introduced her to the employees, fighting the urge to bolt. "I want to, Dad, I do…but I never really did. I don't roll out of bed, charged up about writing ads or designing brochures, and maybe I just need more time to get there. But I am committed, and I'll work hard so you don't have to worry—"

He put a hand on her arm, cutting off her words. "Do you know why I pushed so hard to get you to work for me?"

"To advance the legacy and carry on what you started."

She'd heard the words so often she could recite them in her sleep.

"To see you for more than a week out of the year."

He'd done it to see her? She'd *been* there, and he'd never been there with her. She'd grown up with him. At the end of every day, she'd waited for her father to come tuck her in or read her a story instead of sending the babysitter to do it. Or to go along on a field trip, or a college tour, anything that normal parents did with their children. Instead, he'd been at work, putting that company first, time and time again.

All the things Lauren had never said, the words she had kept locked behind a wall of wanting her father's approval and love, came rushing forward. "You might have seen me, Dad, but you were never *there* with me. You and I never did a single thing together in all the summers we spent here."

"I worked with you on your summer homework, Lauren. And helped you with your German lessons."

"Exactly my point. That was work, too, not vacation. We never went to the beach. We never went to the aquarium. We never got an ice cream downtown."

Impatience filled her father's voice. "I hardly see the relevance of that."

"Because life isn't meant to be spent in an office, Dad." She shook her head. He really was a stubborn man. A great trait when it came to warring with the competition, but not good when it came to relationships. Of course, Carter would argue she'd inherited some of that stubbornness from her

SUMMER LOVE: TAKE TWO

father. If she had, she was going to put it to good use now, because protecting Paradise Key mattered to her. And so did her father.

"Come with me." Lauren put out her hand.

"Where?"

She sighed. "Does it matter? Spend some time with your daughter. And not to talk about work or the company or the marketing plan for Paradise Key. Just time."

Her father gave her a dubious glance, but took her hand. "Okay. I only have—"

"One daughter and whatever time she wants to spend with you." Lauren gave her father a stern look, then led him across the street and down the wooden walkway to the beach. When they reached the sand, she said, "Take off your shoes. Please."

He rolled his eyes, but did as she said. Lauren kicked off her sneakers, then took her father's hand again. They walked down the cool sand to the ocean without saying a word. To the same place Lauren had started her time in Paradise Key a few days ago.

The water washed in and out with the same *shush-shush* song. The tide was coming in, and the water swirled in eddies that divoted into the sand. The moon sent sparkles of light onto the dark water.

"Put your toes in the water, Dad."

"Lauren, we have work—"

She put up a palm to cut off his sentence. "You promised. Now please, put your toes in the water and just…be. For five seconds. For me. Please."

He sighed again, but did as she asked. When the water hit his pants cuffs, she bent down and rolled the material up his ankles. She raised her gaze to her father, leaving her hands on his bare feet for a moment longer. He stayed rigid and still, as if he was unsure what to do with this new daughter who grabbed his hand and kept his pant cuffs from getting wetter.

In all the years Lauren had lived with and worked with her father, they had rarely touched. An obligatory hug after graduation or a funeral for a family member, and nothing more. She'd grown up in a home devoid of physical contact, and so had her widowed father. He'd become a stoic, cold man who focused on facts and figures rather than people and emotions.

And now he was sick and stubborn enough to go through that alone, without the support of the people around him. If there was ever a time for Lauren to find common ground with her father, it was now.

Lauren rose, and clasping her father's hand again. "When is it going to be enough?" she said softly.

"What are you talking about?"

"When are you going to pause for a second and enjoy your life instead of landing one more account, getting one more notch in your belt?" As she said the words, she realized she sounded a lot like Carter. All along, Carter had been trying to get her to see the value of actually living. That was what she'd had a taste of that summer, but as soon as it was gone, she'd retreated to school and work. She had become, in many respects, her father. And as she looked at him now and saw the exhaustion in his eyes, the trembling wall that held his emotions in check, and the strong spine of denial, she realized she was done doing that. "You're sick, Dad. And no company, no account, no client is going to matter if I...if I lose you."

"This water is cold." He started to turn away, but she held tight.

"No, it's not. You're avoiding the conversation."

"We have work to do."

"For God's sake, Dad, the work can wait!" She was tired of dancing around the truth. Of pretending she was content with her life, with their relationship. "Stay here for five minutes and talk to me."

"I can't. Don't you see that? I can't." Her father glanced away and let out a curse. "I have a legacy and people to provide for and—"

Again, the company first. Ahead of his daughter, ahead of his disease, ahead of everything that mattered. "Dad, you have cancer, damn it. When is that going to take precedence?"

"I can't...I can't." He shook his head. "I need to rebuild the company and..."

In the silence after his voice trailed off, Lauren realized

the truth. She kept holding on to her father's hand, but now her touch was softer, gentler. At some point, his fingers had curled over hers. "You're scared, aren't you?"

"Of course not." But his voice trembled as he said it, and the man who had been the most stoic person she'd ever known began to pale.

Her father had avoided talking about the diagnosis and treatment, because he didn't have to face it if it wasn't spoken aloud. He had done the same thing after her mother's death—moving on and going back to work as if nothing had happened. "It's okay to be scared, Dad. It's okay to admit you can't do it all. And it's okay to take a break."

"If I do that, if I slow down..." He stood in the water for a long time, facing the endless black ocean and the stars that twinkled above him. He kept holding his daughter's hand, and she stayed close, her bare feet side by side with his. "If I slow down, Lauren, I'll have to face all those things I never face. What losing your mother did to me, because I didn't realize how much she meant until after it was too late. What this damned disease is doing to me. How I've let you down as a father, and how I should have told you a long time ago how damned proud I am of you, instead of being so hard on you. And how I'm going to...leave you. I don't want to do that."

It was the most emotion her father had ever showed her. All her life, Lauren had wondered if her father loved her. If she was living up to his expectations. Now she looked into his eyes and saw a man who was terrified of losing the only family he had—one who was filled with regret.

"Then don't." She squeezed his hand. "Sell the company. Move down here. Take on a couple of projects a year, but only if you want to. You have enough money, and there are doctors here. I don't want a damned legacy, Dad. I want time with you. Real time."

Her father considered her words for a long moment. "What would we do with that time?"

Lauren leaned her head on his shoulder. "Talk. Walk on the beach. Take a real vacation."

He chuckled, and a lightness she had never seen before filled his face. "I don't think I know how to do that."

"I'll show you, Dad." She wrapped her arm around his waist, and he wrapped his around her. Her father drew her tight against him and pressed a kiss to her forehead, as if she was six and crying over a skinned knee. Lauren's eyes filled. This was what mattered. This was *all* that mattered. "I'll show you."

CARTER WAS A serious glutton for punishment. He spent the next day at work organizing shelves that didn't need organizing, and dusting cans that didn't need dusting. When his father came in that afternoon, Carter had opted to work in the back of the store, organizing the storage area, instead of talking about why he was in such a foul mood.

Lauren had probably gone back to New York. And he was already miserable. He'd let her go once before, and had never found another woman who intrigued him like she did. Now she was leaving again, and he was—

An idiot.

He thought of what his father had done to win his mother. How hard the two of them worked to keep their relationship strong. Was he really going to let a little thing like a thousand miles keep them apart?

Later that day, Jacob Evans came into the store. Carter's father was at the bank getting change for the register, so Carter dusted off his hands and went out to the front. "What can I get you, Mr. Evans?"

"Well, I'm gonna need another bottle of wine. And one of those frozen cakes, if you have them."

"We do." Carter retrieved the cake from the freezer case and put it on the counter, then snagged a bottle of Jacob's favorite wine and set it beside the cake. "What's the occasion this time? Another date?"

"Nope. I'm done dating." Jacob's nod added punctuation to his sentence. "I found everything I could want already."

Carter rang up the purchase, then made change for a twenty and handed the bills to Jacob. "And who's the lucky lady?"

"Gladys." Jacob beamed, and his smile could have been

that of a man fifty years younger. He almost glowed with happiness. "We had dinner after we volunteered at Lynette's the other night, and she made her lasagna. Best damned lasagna in the state, and I made the mistake of saying hers was better than Anna's. Well, Gladys didn't take too kindly to finding out I was courting Anna, too. She dumped that platter right in my lap, then told me that she's not the kind of woman who shares her man. Just before she kicked me out, she said if I wanted to be her man, then I'd better step up to the plate." He chuckled. "I haven't had a woman put me in my place like that since my wife died in eighty-six, God rest her soul."

Jacob had described Gladys as a firecracker, and Carter could see why. He put the wine into a paper bag, then nestled it beside the cake in a second, larger bag. "And you think a cake and some wine is going to be enough?"

"Hell no. I bought her some jewelry, too. And I have a bouquet of roses in the car. I'm going to march up to her door right now and tell her that if she wants to be my woman, she better make an honest man out of me." Jacob picked up the bag. "Wish me luck."

Carter chuckled. "You have quite the way with the ladies of Paradise Key, Mr. Evans. I don't think you're going to need any luck."

"Ah, but that's where you're wrong, young man. Women like Gladys don't come along every day. If she says yes, I'm going to count my lucky stars, and then make sure she knows

I love her every day for the rest of her life." Jacob turned to go, then pivoted back. "When you find the woman who makes you crazier than you've ever been, the one woman you can't forget no matter how hard you try, you better damned well scoop her up. And then, son, you'll be lucky, too."

The door gave a happy jingle as Jacob left. He nodded toward Carter's dad, then got into his car and pulled away.

"Was that Jacob Evans?" Roger asked when he came back into the store.

"Yep. Apparently, he's going to propose to Gladys tonight."

His father laughed. "I'm glad. I've seen the two of them together. She's one of the few people who can keep him in line. And she's also one heck of a nice woman."

"That's pretty much what Jacob said. He also told me not to let the woman who makes me crazy get away. That if I can't stop thinking about her, she's the one, and I'd be a lucky man if she said yes."

"And that is why I think Jacob Evans is one of the wisest men in Paradise Key." Roger opened the cash drawer to add more quarters and dimes, then exchanged a twenty for a stack of one-dollar bills. "He said something similar to me years ago when I was hemming and hawing about your mom. He was happily married then, and boy, did he love his wife. It was a shame when he lost her. We were all worried he'd never be the same. It's nice to see him find happiness again."

Carter nodded. He wandered around the store for a little while, his mind churning over what his father and Jacob had said. "Dad, would you mind closing tonight?"

"Wait, you were at work today? Because all I've been hearing all day is swearing and cans moving." His dad chuckled. "Of course I can close. I'm hoping it's so you can go see the one woman who drives you crazy? Because you look a lot like I did after I saw Hank McLeary with your mother. Are things rocky with Lauren?"

"They are. But they won't be for long." He gave his dad a quick hug. "I'm taking a page out of the Malone and Evans playbooks and going for the big gesture. The biggest one I can make."

His father arched a brow. "You have a ring?"

"No, but…" Carter glanced around the store, as if an engagement ring would materialize. "Well, maybe I can do that part later. I don't know. All I know is if I don't do something now, Lauren is going to go back to New York and I'm not going to let her leave without trying again."

"Good luck." His father clapped him on the back. "I'm proud of the man you have become, son."

"I had a great example to follow." Carter gave his father a quick hug, then headed out of the store. He drove across town, then parked in the lot for the little place where Lauren had been staying while she was in Paradise Key. Lauren's car was still there. Thank goodness.

He headed inside the building, stopping at the desk to

talk to the owner long enough to ask for Lauren's room—one of the benefits to living in a small town was the owner being a good friend—then charged up the stairs to the second floor. He knocked, then held his breath until Lauren opened the door.

"Carter. What are you doing here?" She was barefoot, wearing only a pale pink T-shirt and a pair of pink plaid pajama pants. Her hair was down, her face bare, and she looked so damned beautiful he almost forgot why he was there.

"Asking you a question." He leaned against the doorjamb. "Do you love me?"

Confusion filled her features. "What kind of question is that?"

"Do you love me?" He was pretty confident in her answer, but still, his heart stayed in his throat, and the seconds she took to reply seemed interminable. He'd never cared so much about how a woman felt. Not with his fiancée in Chicago, or with any of the other women who had come after Lauren. It had always been Lauren, ever since he'd seen her in the ice cream parlor that summer and fell in love with the way her eyes lit when he dared her to sneak off in the middle of the night.

She raised her gaze to his and held the connection, her green eyes deep as a forest. "You know I do. I always have."

Hope soared in his chest. "Good. Then prove it." He grinned, leaning toward her. "Meet me on the beach tonight.

As soon as possible, because I don't want to wait ten years for you again."

Then he turned and left, praying the whole way that history would repeat itself.

Chapter Twelve

THIS TIME, LAUREN Webster didn't climb out of the window or sneak past her sleeping aunt. She left the Airbnb by the back door that opened to the lawn. She didn't bother to get dressed or put on shoes. She knew what she wanted, and ten years was too long to wait to finally go after it.

All this time, she had been stubbornly holding on to the security of work. Because there, like her father, she could bury her head in the sand and not face the mistakes she had made or the regrets that haunted her nights. After she'd talked to her father last night, then enjoyed a day in Paradise Key with him today, seeing the sights, walking the beach, strolling through downtown, the two of them had begun building a relationship. The conversation had gone in fits and starts, with each of them retreating to the common ground of work, but as the day wore on and they ran out of work things to talk about, their words had turned more personal. She had told him how much she had missed him growing up, but how much she admired what he had done with the company.

He apologized for pushing her so hard, for demanding so

much. "You really aren't happy in this job, are you?" he asked.

Lauren paused, and then she nodded. When she said, "no," it was as if a weight had been lifted off her shoulders. All those years of trying to fit into a world she didn't enjoy had taken a toll she hadn't even realized just then.

And then her father fired her.

Well, he didn't fire her so much as tell her to go after what she really wanted. "You'll have my support, because I think it's about time I asked you what you wanted from your life rather than dictating it."

"And you'll have mine," she said with tears in her eyes. Her father nodded, a bit choked up himself, then he said he'd treat her to an ice cream. They shared a dish of chocolate chip as the afternoon wound to a close, then headed back to the Airbnb, where an extra room had opened for her father to rent. Gerald went to bed early, and Lauren had been pacing her room, debating her next move when Carter showed up and gave her the answer she needed. Her next move, she thought as she slipped outside, was with Carter. Whatever that meant.

Lauren ran across the dewy grass, then down the cool sand. She skidded to a stop when she saw a giant heart drawn in the sand, then a second one intersecting it. And in between the hearts, there was Carter, down on one knee.

Oh my God. Was he doing what she thought he was doing? When she'd said to herself that she didn't want to wait any longer, had she meant marriage? The idea both thrilled and terrified her.

"I have a new campaign idea for you," he said as he opened his fist. Something shiny sat on his palm.

Okay, so this wasn't a proposal. The thought was more disappointment than relief. She'd thought maybe she and Carter…

There was no sense traveling down that mental road. Whatever he was doing here tonight was about the marketing campaign. That was what she wanted, wasn't it? Or what she used to want, before she'd gone and fallen in love with Carter Malone all over again. Now, the realization he wasn't asking her to marry him sank a heavy stone in her gut.

Lauren took a step closer to Carter and dropped her eyes. A *Welcome to Paradise Key* keyring sat in his hand. Shaped like the state of Florida, the colorful keyring was the kind of thing tourists bought and forgot. And exactly the kind of kitschy, tacky thing Carter had said he didn't want to use to promote the town. Had she stepped into an alternate universe? "Uh, keyrings?"

"No. *A* ring. Well, a sort of ring. I'll get a real ring tomorrow. I was kind of in a hurry tonight."

She shook her head. "I'm confused. Is this about selling Paradise Key to tourists?"

"No, silly. It's about selling me to you." He reached for her hand, then drew her closer. Her heart skipped a beat, and she held her breath as he began to talk. "I realize I have a bad track record for breaking your heart, and you might not believe I won't do it again. But I'm here tonight to sell you on taking a chance on the new and improved Carter Malone. He's still a little rough around the edges, and far from perfect, but he has figured out what he wants. And he's grown up quite a bit since that summer."

Lauren laughed. "Carter 2.0? Is that what you're advertising?"

"Yup. He doesn't come with much of a warranty, but he does promise to…" Carter paused, then drew in a breath. "Love you for the rest of our lives. I love you, Lauren, and I never want to lose you again."

Her heart soared, and all the little lies she'd told herself about not being disappointed earlier were erased. This was what she had wanted, what she had hoped for from the second he showed up at her door. "You still love me?"

"Wait, did I forget to say that earlier?" He grinned. "Yes, Lauren, I love you. I never stopped. And now, I want to marry you. I'll move to New York, or Timbuktu, as long as we're together."

"I don't want you to move to New York with me. Or Timbuktu."

His face fell. He started to get up, but Lauren put a hand on his shoulder. "I'm not leaving you, Carter. I'm not leaving Paradise Key at all."

"You're not?"

She shook her head, and the smile she'd been holding

back spread across her face. "Well, I will have to leave for a couple of weeks so I can sublet my New York apartment and pack my things. But after that, I'm coming down here to stay, and so is my father. For a permanent vacation for him, and a new venture for me."

"A new venture?" Smiling up at her, he placed the keyring into her hand, then closed her fingers over it. His dark eyes met hers. The moon sparkled in his eyes, on his smile. "If you don't mind a slightly unprepared proposal, I want to ask you…" He took in another breath, then held her gaze, his face serious and firm and hopeful. "Lauren, will you marry me?"

She looked at the keyring. At the colorful state of Florida dangling off a silver circle. And the man before her, waiting for an answer. Ironic he'd chosen a keyring, because those were often tied to new journeys. New homes. New adventures. "I already know my answer, Carter. I've been holding onto it for ten years. Yes. Yes to a whatever our future holds, yes to getting married, and yes to us."

A wide grin spread across his face. He scrambled to his feet, drew her into his arms, and kissed her. It was a sweet kiss, a loving kiss, the kind that made her feel treasured and precious and loved. The kind of kiss she had been searching for all those years since she left Paradise Key, and hadn't realized was waiting for her down here all this time.

Afterward, she leaned her head on Carter's chest and listened to his heart beat. The sound matched the soft song of the ocean as it rolled in, a new tide washing the beach clean and beginning again. This...this was paradise.

"I'm home," she whispered. "Finally."

"Me too, Lauren," he said, dancing the words across her temple, then drawing her to him for one more kiss, and one more moment under the stars.

Epilogue

THE LITTLE HOUSE sat close to the beach, just a two-block walk along quiet streets. Lauren grabbed some sunscreen, a couple of water bottles, and a pair of beach towels, then stuffed them in a big canvas bag she threw over her shoulder. "Are you ready yet, honey?"

"Yep." Carter strode into the kitchen, moving to wrap his arms around Lauren's waist. His wedding ring glinted in the sun streaming through the windows. "I gotta say I love this new bikini. I loved the pink one. And the blue one. But this white one...I'm not sure how long we're going to stay at the beach, because I'm going to want to run back here and take it off you. Or maybe...leave it on." He waggled his eyebrows playfully.

She laughed, turning her face to kiss him. "We're going to be late, Romeo. We'll have plenty of time for that after we get back."

"Okay, okay." He planted a kiss on her shoulder, then released her to pick up the cooler sitting by the back door. "Let's go. That means you, too, Nutter Butter."

Their golden retriever, still gangly and clumsy at nine months old, came bounding out of the living room. She stood by the door, tail wagging a hundred times a minute while Carter attached the leash.

"Every time I hear you call that dog, it cracks me up," Lauren said.

"Ah, but I still get brownie points for the best birthday present ever, right?"

"Honey, you get brownie points just for marrying me." She kissed him again, then forgot about leaving for a moment when Carter's arm stole around her waist and he deepened their kiss. "Okay, so maybe we can be a little late."

He laughed, then opened the door. Nutter Butter bounded forward, nearly yanking Carter's arm out of the socket. "I'd love to be late, but everyone's waiting."

They headed down the street, their flip-flops slapping against the pavement. When they reached the small boardwalk leading from the neighborhood down to the water, Carter and Lauren kicked off their shoes, then walked down the soft, cool sand toward a wide bright orange umbrella.

As she neared the group sitting in the beach chairs under the umbrella, Lauren whispered a prayer of gratitude. A year ago, she never would have imagined she would be here, in Paradise Key, surrounded by those she loved. In another week, all the girls would be here, for a happier reunion than the last one, a small one-year later celebration on the beach. She couldn't wait to see Jenna, Evie, and Sofia, and catch up with all the wonderful changes in their lives, too.

Carter's parents sat in two of the beach chairs, a cooler

between them serving as a table for their lunch and a couple of sodas. On the other side of Roger, Lauren's father sat in a bright green beach chair, looking relaxed and at ease. He'd foregone the suits a few months ago, and now had a big collection of shorts and loud Hawaiian shirts that he said made him look like a local. He had color in his cheeks and hope in his heart, and Lauren told him often that Paradise Key was to credit for the improvement in his health. Today, they were going to celebrate the news that his cancer was in remission, and that her father had been given a new life. One he was determined to live in new ways. He'd left the company in the hands of the other partners, and did the occasional consultation with a client, but made sure he only worked a handful of hours a week.

Carter drew Lauren to a halt a few feet away from their families. "I'm so incredibly happy," he said. "Our lives are more amazing than I even imagined they would be."

"How could they not be? We live in a place named Paradise." Rising on her tiptoes, she kissed her husband while the dog dashed around their legs and twined them together with the leash. She heard their families laugh while the sun above smiled warmth and her husband loved her with all of his heart. Lauren thought of the cocktail napkin and that evening in the bar. Little did she know she'd been writing the perfect slogan for the future that had been waiting for her. And now, her life was perfect...for all the right reasons.

The End

The Paradise Key Series

After the sudden death of one of their friends, four single women who spent their summers at a beachside resort with their families return. The place they loved when they were young is falling apart, as are the lives of the four women. They each have their own reasons for returning, and their own secrets to keep. But as they bond together to restore a bit of their past, they find love in the beachside town, and the happiness they have sought all their lives.

Book 1: *Summer Love: Take Two* by Shirley Jump

Book 2: *Love at the Beach Shop* by Kyra Jacobs

Book 3: *Resort to Love* by Priscilla Oliveras

Book 4: *Small Town Love* by Susan Meier

Available now at your favorite online retailer!

About the Author

When she's not writing books, New York Times and USA Today bestselling author Shirley Jump competes in triathlons, mostly because all that training lets her justify mid-day naps and a second slice of chocolate cake. She's published more than 60 books in 24 languages, although she's too geographically challenged to find any of those countries on a map.

Visit her website at shirleyjump.com for author news and a booklist, and follow her on Facebook at facebook.com/shirleyjump.author for giveaways and deep discussions about important things like chocolate and shoes.

Thank you for reading

Summer Love: Take Two

If you enjoyed this book, you can find more from all our great authors at TulePublishing.com, or from your favorite online retailer.

TULE
PUBLISHING

76516333R00116

Made in the USA
Middletown, DE
13 June 2018